DANGEROUS DUKES

Rakes about town

Carole Mortimer introduces London's
most delectable dukes in her new mini-series.

But don't be fooled by their charm,
because beneath their lazy smiles they're
deliciously sexy—and highly dangerous!

Coming this month

DARIAN HUNTER: DUKE OF DESIRE

And don't miss the first in this mini-series

ZACHARY BLACK:
DUKE OF DEBAUCHERY

Available now

Or the online prequel

MARCUS WILDING:
DUKE OF PLEASURE

Mariah held back the hysterical laugh that threatened to burst forth at the obvious sincerity of Darian's promise of allowing no harm to come to her—when the person she now feared the most was *him*.

Oh, not him, exactly, but her responses to him certainly. Responses of heat and desire. Responses which she had believed herself to be incapable of feeling towards any man.

Until Wolfingham.

Just a few minutes of being back in his company and Mariah had known that she was still aware of everything about him. The dark and glossy thickness of his hair. Those beautiful emerald-green eyes. The stark and chiselled handsomeness of his features. The strength of his muscled body.

The gentleness of the long and sensitive hands that now held her hands so lightly, but securely, within his own.

Hands that Mariah could only too easily imagine moving, exploring her body, lighting a fire wherever they touched, giving pleasure wherever they caressed. A pleasure she'd never imagined she could desire so deeply…

DARIAN HUNTER: DUKE OF DESIRE

Carole Mortimer

First published in Great Britain 2014
by Mills & Boon, an imprint of Harlequin (UK) Limited,
Large Print edition 2015
Harlequin (UK) Limited, Eton House, 18-24 Paradise Road,
Richmond, Surrey TW9 1SR

© 2014 Carole Mortimer

ISBN: 978-0-263-25532-4

Harlequin (UK) Limited's policy is to use papers that are natural,
renewable and recyclable products and made from wood grown in
sustainable forests. The logging and manufacturing processes conform
to the legal environmental regulations of the country of origin.

Printed and bound in Great Britain
by CPI Antony Rowe, Chippenham, Wiltshire

Carole Mortimer was born in England, the youngest of three children. She began writing in 1978, and has now written over one hundred and fifty books for Harlequin Mills & Boon®. Carole has six sons: Matthew, Joshua, Timothy, Michael, David and Peter. She says, 'I'm happily married to Peter senior; we're best friends as well as lovers, which is probably the best recipe for a successful relationship. We live in a lovely part of England.'

Previous novels by the same author:

In Mills & Boon® Historical Romance:

THE DUKE'S CINDERELLA BRIDE*
THE RAKE'S WICKED PROPOSAL*
THE ROGUE'S DISGRACED LADY*
LADY ARABELLA'S SCANDALOUS MARRIAGE*
CHRISTMAS AT MULBERRY HALL
   (part of *Regency Christmas Proposals* anthology)
THE LADY GAMBLES**
THE LADY FORFEITS**
THE LADY CONFESSES**
SOME LIKE IT WICKED†
SOME LIKE TO SHOCK†
NOT JUST A GOVERNESS††
NOT JUST A WALLFLOWER††
ZACHARY BLACK: DUKE OF DEBAUCHERY+

**The Notorious St Claires*
***The Copeland Sisters*
†*Daring Duchesses*
††*A Season of Secrets*
+*Dangerous Dukes*

And in Mills & Boon® Historical *Undone!* eBooks:

AT THE DUKE'S SERVICE
CONVENIENT WIFE, PLEASURED LADY
A WICKEDLY PLEASURABLE WAGER**
SOME LIKE IT SCANDALOUS†
NOT JUST A SEDUCTION††
MARCUS WILDING: DUKE OF PLEASURE+

And in M&B Regency *Castonbury Park* mini-series:

THE WICKED LORD MONTAGUE

**Did you know that some of these novels
are also available as eBooks?
Visit www.millsandboon.co.uk**

DEDICATION

My good friend, Susan Stephens.
What fun we have on our travels!

Prologue

'You wanted to speak to me?'

Having been perusing today's newspaper, whilst seated in an otherwise deserted private room of his club, Darian Hunter, the Duke of Wolfingham, now continued reading to the end of the article before folding the broadsheet neatly into four and placing it down on the low table beside him. He then glanced up at the fashionably dressed young gentleman who had addressed him so aggressively. 'And a good afternoon to you, too, Anthony,' he greeted his younger brother calmly.

Anthony eyed him impatiently. 'Do not come the haughty duke with me, Darian! Most especially when I know it is you who wished to speak with me rather than the other way about. You have left messages for me all over town,' he reminded as Darian raised dark brows questioningly. 'I presumed the matter must be of some urgency?'

'Is that why it has taken you those same two days to respond to those messages?' Darian was not fooled for a moment by his brother's bluster. He knew that his brother always went on the attack when he knew he was in the wrong, but was refusing to admit it.

'I have better things to do with my time than seek out the more often than not elusive Duke of Wolfingham—even if he does happen to be my big brother as well as my guardian. The latter for only another three months, I thank heavens!'

'Oh, do sit down, Anthony,' Darian snapped. 'You are making the place look untidy.'

Anthony gave a wicked grin at having obviously succeeded in irritating Darian as he threw himself down into the chair opposite. He was dressed in the height of fashion as usual, in his jacket of royal blue, with a bright blue-and-green paisley-patterned waistcoat beneath and buff-coloured pantaloons, his dark hair rakishly over-long and falling across his brow. 'When did you get back to town?'

'Two days ago, obviously,' Darian drawled.

'And you immediately sought me out?' Anthony raised mocking brows. 'I am flattered, brother.'

'Don't be,' he advised pointedly.

His brother now raised his gaze heavenwards. 'What have I done to annoy you this time? Over-spent at my tailor's? Gambled at the cards a little too heavily?'

'If only it was your usual irresponsible behaviour then I should not have needed to speak with you at all, but merely dealt with the matter as I always do,' Darian drawled in a bored voice. 'I am sure we are both well aware of why it is I wished to speak with you, Anthony,' he added softly.

'Not the slightest idea.' The fact that Anthony shifted uncomfortably, his gaze now avoiding meeting Darian's as a slight flush coloured his cheeks, instantly gave lie to the claim.

Darian gave a humourless smile. 'Do not force me to mention the lady by name.'

Anthony narrowed eyes as emerald green as Darian's own, the two of them very alike in colouring and looks, and so obviously brothers, in spite of the eight years' difference in their ages; Darian aged two and thirty to his brother's four and twenty. 'If you are referring to the actress with whom I had a liaison last month, then I do not even recall her name—'

'I am not.'

Anthony gave an exaggerated stretch of his shoulders. 'Then give me a clue, brother, because I have absolutely no idea what—or possibly who?—you might be referring to.'

Darian's mouth firmed at his brother's determination not to make this an easy conversation. For either of them. 'It has been brought to my attention that you have been seen in the company of a certain lady, more often than is socially acceptable.'

Anthony stilled. 'Indeed?'

Darian nodded. 'And while it is perfectly acceptable for you to discreetly indulge in a gentleman's diversions, this particular lady could never be considered as being in the least discreet. Indeed, she is—'

'Have a care, Darian,' Anthony warned softly.

'Her associations, past and present, mean she is not a woman with whom it is acceptable for a gentleman of your standing to indulge in these diversions,' Darian maintained determinedly. 'You—' He broke off as Anthony sprang lightly to his feet, hands clenched into fists at his sides as he glared down at Darian. 'I have not finished—'

'In regard to this particular lady, I assure you that you have indeed finished,' Anthony said fiercely. 'And might I say that you have a damned nerve, daring to lecture me about my behaviour, when you have only just returned from spending almost two weeks in the company of whatever doxy it was who had so taken your fancy you might have disappeared off the edge of the earth! Or perhaps it is that you consider a duke is allowed to live by different standards than us mere mortals?'

Darian lowered heavy lids as he flicked an

imaginary speck of lint from the sleeve of his jacket, at the same time avoiding meeting his brother's accusing gaze.

Not because he had just spent almost two weeks with his latest doxy. 'Latest doxy'? Darian could not even remember the last time he had spent any length of time in a woman's company, let alone her bed.

No, the reason for his avoidance of Anthony's probing gaze was because he had not been in a woman's company at all, but had spent almost two weeks across the sea in France, acting secretly as an agent for the Crown.

Almost two weeks when he and his good friend Zachary Black, the Duke of Hawksmere, had roamed the French countryside, and then Paris itself, as they endeavoured to gauge how the French people themselves felt about Napoleon's return, the emperor having recently escaped from Elba and currently on his way to the French capital.

Not even Darian's own brother was aware of the work he had undertaken for the Crown these past five years. Anthony certainly had no idea that Darian had suffered a bullet wound to the shoulder just days ago, a souvenir of this last foray into France. And that he was suffering with the pain and discomfort of that wound even now.

Something that had not improved his temper in the slightest. 'Perhaps you would care to lower your voice?'

'Why should I, when there is no one else here to hear us?' Anthony challenged as he looked about the otherwise empty room.

Darian sighed. 'I am well aware that this lady has certain attributes that you—most gentlemen!—might find diverting. But she is not a discreet woman. Far from it, if gossip is to be believed. People in society are starting to comment upon your marked attentions to her.'

'Then let them,' Anthony dismissed with bravado.

He sighed. 'It simply will not do, Anthony.'

'Says who? You?' his brother challenged, aggressive once again. 'I am almost five and twenty, Darian, not five. Nor,' he added darkly, 'do I appreciate your interference in this matter.'

'Even when I have your best interests at heart?'

'Not when I am in love with the lady, no.'

Darian held on to his temper with difficulty, having had no idea that his brother's affections had become engaged to such a degree. A physical diversion, if discreetly handled, was acceptable; a love affair most certainly was not. 'I am sure the lady has certain charms and experience, which you obviously find attractive. But it would be a mistake on your part to confuse lust with love.'

'How dare you?' Anthony challenged fiercely, his face having become a mottled and angry red. 'My intentions towards the lady are completely honourable!'

Then it was worse even than Darian had feared. 'By all means continue to bed her then, Anthony, if that is your wish. All I am asking is that you at least try to make less of the association when the two of you are in public.'

'Continue to—' Anthony looked as if he might now explode with the depth of his fury. 'I have not laid so much as an indelicate finger upon the lady. Nor do I intend to do so until after I have made her my wife.'

Now it was Darian's turn to stand up, his shock at this announcement too great to be contained. 'You cannot even think of making such a woman your wife!'

'Such a woman? You damned hypocritical prig!' Anthony glared at him, eyes glittering darkly. 'You return from who knows where, after spending days, almost two weeks, in some woman's bed, and you have the nerve to tell me how I might conduct my own life. Whom I may or may not marry! Well, I shall have none of it, Darian,' he dismissed heatedly. 'In just a few more weeks I shall have control of my own life and my own fortune, and when I do I shall marry whom, and when, I damn well please.'

Darian gave an impatient shake of his head. 'This particular woman is—'

'A darling. An angel.' His brother's voice rose angrily. 'And it is as well you have chosen not to so much as say her name, because your conversation today shows you are not fit to do so.'

Darian winced. From all that he had heard of the lady, she was neither a darling nor an angel. Far from it.

Nor did he have any intentions of allowing his brother to marry such a woman.

And if Anthony could not be made to see sense, then the lady must…

Chapter One

Two days later—the ballroom of Carlisle House, London

'Would you care to repeat your remark, Wolfingham, for I fear the music and loud chatter must have prevented me from hearing you correctly the first time?'

Darian did not need to look down, into the face of the woman with whom he was dancing, to know Mariah Beecham, widowed Countess of Carlisle, *had* heard him correctly the first time; her displeasure was more than obvious, in both the frosty tone of her voice and the stiffness of her elegantly clad body.

'I doubt that very much, madam,' he drawled just as icily, as the two of them continued to smile for the benefit of any watching them as they moved about the dance floor, in perfect sequence with the other couples dancing. 'Nevertheless, I will gladly repeat my statement, in that it is my wish that you immediately cease to encourage my brother in this ridiculous infatuation he seems to have developed for you.'

'The implication being that you believe me to have been deliberately encouraging those attentions in the first place?' His hostess for the evening arched one haughty blonde brow over eyes of an exquisite and unusual shade of turquoise blue.

A colour that Darian had previously only associated with the Mediterranean Sea, on a clear summer's day.

Darian had long been aware of this lady's presence in society, of course, first as the Earl of Carlisle's much younger wife and, for these past five years, as that deceased gentleman's very wealthy and scandalous widow.

But this was the first occasion upon which Darian had spent any length of time in her company. Having done so, he now perfectly understood his younger brother's infatuation with the countess; she was, without doubt, a woman of unparalleled beauty.

Her hair was the gold of ripened corn, her complexion as pale and smooth as alabaster; a creamy brow, softly curving cheeks, her neck long, with elegantly plump shoulders shown to advantage by the low *décolletage* of her gown. Those unusual turquoise eyes were surrounded by thick dark lashes, her nose small and pert above generous—and sensual—lips and the ampleness of her breasts revealed above a silk gown of the same deep turquoise colour as her eyes.

No, Darian could not fault his brother's taste in women, for Mariah Beecham was a veritable diamond, in regard to both her beauty and those voluptuous breasts.

Unfortunately, she was also a widow aged four and thirty to Anthony's only four and twenty, and mother to a daughter of seventeen. Indeed her daughter, the Lady Christina Beecham, was newly out this Season, and so also present this evening. She also bore a startling physical resemblance to her mother.

The young Lady Christina Beecham did not, however, as yet have the same scandalous reputation as her mother.

It was that reputation that had prompted Darian's recent concerns in regard to his brother's future happiness and for him to have uncharacteristically decided to interfere in the association.

He would have understood if Anthony had merely wished to discreetly share the lady's bed for a few weeks, or possibly even months. He accepted that all young gentlemen indulged in these sexual diversions—indeed, he had done so himself for many years at that age—for their own enjoyment and in order to gain the physical experience considered necessary for the marriage bed.

Unfortunately, this lady could never be called discreet. And Anthony had made it more than plain, in their conversation two days ago, that he did not regard Mariah Beecham as his mere mistress.

As Anthony's older brother and only relation, Darian could not allow him to entertain such a ruinous marriage. As Anthony's guardian, for at least another few months and so still in control of Anthony's considerable fortune, Darian considered it to be nothing more than an unsuitable infatuation.

His efforts so far to dissuade Anthony from continuing in his pursuit of this woman had been to no avail; his brother could be as stubborn as Darian when he had decided on a course of action.

Consequently, Darian had been left with no choice but to approach and speak to the woman herself, and he had attended the countess's ball this evening for just that purpose. His forays into polite society had been rare these past few years.

He much preferred to spend his evenings at his private club, or gambling establishments, in the company of the four gentlemen who had been his closest friends since their schooldays together. The past ten years had seen the five of them become known collectively in society as The Dangerous Dukes. It was a reputation they had earned for their exploits in the bedchamber, albeit discreetly in recent years, as much as on the battlefield.

Confirmed bachelors all, Darian had recently watched as two of his close friends had succumbed to falling in love—one of them had already married, the second was well on his way to being so.

Much as he might deplore the distance a wife would necessarily put between himself and two of his closest friends, Darian considered the two ladies in question to be more than suitable as his friends' consorts, and had no doubt that both ladies were equally as smitten as his two friends and that the marriages would flourish.

Also, Worthing and Hawksmere were both gentlemen aged two and thirty, the same age as Darian himself, and so both old enough, he considered, to know their own minds, and hearts. His brother, Anthony, was so much younger, and as such Darian did not consider him old enough as yet to know enough of life, let alone the true meaning of love for any woman.

Most especially, he knew Anthony could have no previous experience with a woman of Mariah Beecham's age and reputation. Nor had it helped to quell Darian's disquiet over the association that, when he had arrived here earlier this evening, his first sighting of his younger brother had been as he danced with the countess, a besotted smile upon his youthfully handsome face!

That she now felt just as strongly opposed as Anthony did to Darian's interference in the friendship was in no doubt as he looked down into those cold and challenging turquoise eyes.

It was a long time since Mariah had allowed anyone to anger her to the degree Darian Hunter had just succeeded in doing. Not since her husband, Martin, had been alive, in fact. But Darian Hunter, the arrogantly superior Duke of Wolfingham, had undoubtedly succeeded in annoying her intensely.

How dared this man come into her home and chastise her in this way? As if she were no more than a rebellious and impressionable young girl for him to reprove and reproach for her actions?

Actions of which she was, in this particular instance, completely innocent.

Mariah had, of course, been aware of Anthony Hunter's youthful attentions to her during these past few weeks. Attentions that she had neither encouraged nor discouraged. The former, because Anthony could never be any more to her than an entertaining boy, and the latter, because she had not wanted to hurt those youthful feelings.

All of which she would happily have assured his arrogant duke of a brother, if Wolfingham had not been so determined to be unpleasant to her from the moment they began dancing together.

She should have known that Darian Hunter, a gentleman known for his contempt of all polite social occasions, would have an ulterior motive when he had accepted the invitation to her ball. That he had also claimed a dance with her was unheard of; the duke's usual preference was to stand on the edge of society, looking coldly down his haughty nose at them all.

So much for that particular social feather in her cap! For Mariah now knew that Darian Hunter's only reason for attending her ball, for asking her to dance, had been with the intention of being unpleasant to her.

If only he was not so devilishly handsome, Mariah might have found it in her heart to forgive him. After all, his concern for the welfare of his younger brother and ward was commendable; Mariah also felt that same protectiveness in regard to her daughter, Christina.

And Wolfingham's arrogant handsomeness was of a kind that no woman could remain completely immune to it. Not even a woman as jaded as herself.

That she knew she was not immune rankled and irritated Mariah more than any of the insulting things Wolfingham had just said to her.

The duke was excessively tall, at least a foot taller than her own five feet, his overlong hair as black as night and inclined to curl slightly on his brow and about his ears. His face—emerald-green eyes fringed by thick dark lashes, a long patrician nose, sharp blades for cheekbones, with sculptured lips that might have graced a Michelangelo statue, along with a strong and determined jaw—possessed a masculine beauty that was undeniably arresting.

The width of his shoulders, and broad and

powerfully muscled chest, were all also shown to advantage in his perfectly tailored, black evening clothes. As were his lean and muscled thighs, and the long length of his legs and calves.

Wolfingham was, in fact, everything that Mariah, while acknowledging his male splendour, recoiled from and disliked in a man.

'I was not implying anything, madam.' Those sculptured lips now turned back contemptuously. 'Merely stating a fact.'

Mariah eyed him coldly. 'Indecd?'

Wolfingham nodded tersely. 'I know, for example, that my brother has attended every one of the same excessive amount of entertainments as you have these past three weeks or more. That he then rarely leaves your side for longer than a few minutes. That he calls at your home at least three, sometimes four, times a week and that he stays well beyond the time of any of your other callers. And that, in turn, you—'

'You are having me watched?' Mariah gasped, so disturbed at the thought she had almost stumbled in the dance.

'I am having my brother watched,' Wolfingham corrected grimly, his tightened grip upon her gloved hand having prevented her stumble. 'It is an unfortunate…coincidence that you have always happened to be wherever Anthony is and so your own movements have been afforded that same interest.'

It was truly insupportable that the haughtily contemptuous Duke of Wolfingham dared to so blatantly admit to having monitored those innocent meetings. Totally unacceptable on any level Mariah cared to consider and regardless of Wolfingham's reasons for having done so.

Lord Anthony Hunter was young, yes, but surely old enough to live his own life as he chose, without this excessive interference from his arrogant and disapproving older brother?

As for Mariah, she did not care in the least for having her personal life placed under such close scrutiny.

'Well, madam, what is your answer to be to my request?' Darian prompted impatiently, aware that the dance would soon come to an end and having no desire to waste any more of his evening than was absolutely necessary at the countess's ball. His shoulder, still healing from the recent bullet wound, was currently giving him an excessive amount of pain, following his exertions on the dance floor.

Mariah Beecham pulled her hand from his and stepped back and away from him as the dance came to an end. 'My answer is to make a request of my own, which is that *you* should leave my home forthwith!'

Darian's eyes widened in surprise before he was able to hide it; he had been the Marquis of Durham for all of his life, and the Duke of Wolfingham these past seven years, and as such no one talked to him in such a condescending manner as Mariah Beecham had just done.

He did not know whether to be irritated or amused that she should have done so now. 'And if I should choose not to?'

Her smile was again obviously for the benefit of anyone observing them, rather than genuinely meant, her gaze remaining icily cold as she took the arm he offered to lead her from the dance floor. 'In that case I will have no choice but to ask two of my footmen to forcibly remove you,' she answered with insincere sweetness as she removed her hand and turned to face him.

In contrast, Darian's own smile was perfectly sincere. Indeed, he could not remember being this amused and entertained, by anyone or anything, in a very long time. If ever! 'Are you certain two footmen would be sufficient to the task?' he drawled derisively.

An angry flush coloured those alabaster cheeks at his obvious mockery. 'I do not care how many footmen it takes, your Grace, as long as they are successful in removing you, and your insulting presence, from my home.' Her voluptuous breasts quickly rose and fell in her agitation.

'I believe I have only been stating the obvious, madam.' Darian arched a challenging brow.

'Which is that you consider me entirely unsuitable as a focus for your brother's infatuation?'

'I would go further, madam, and say that I find you entirely unsuitable to occupy any situation in my brother's life.' Darian's mouth thinned disapprovingly at the realisation that *he* now found himself in the position of being attracted to this bewitching woman. A woman, he had discovered during the course of the past few minutes, totally unlike any other he had ever met.

Mariah Beecham was undoubtedly a dazzling beauty and it was impossible for a man's gaze not to admire the rise and fall of those voluptuous and creamy breasts. But he had discovered, as they danced together, that she was far more than just a beautiful face and a desirable body.

Her forthright manner, and her obvious contempt for him, was a refreshing change after the years of women simpering and flirting in his company, in a bid to secure his attention and in the hopes they might one day become his duchess.

Mariah Beecham was obviously a mature and sophisticated woman. A wealthy and independent woman more than capable of making her own decisions as well as bringing up her young daughter alone. Moreover, the countess was a woman who made it perfectly clear that she would do it in exactly the way that *she* pleased.

That sophistication and independence of will was having the strangest effect upon Darian's libido. Indeed, he found himself becoming aroused

grimly as he maintained his hold upon her arm long enough to cross the ballroom and step outside on to the deserted terrace.

He released her arm as abruptly as he had earlier grasped it, before placing both of his hands behind his back and clasping them together as he looked down the length of his nose at her.

'How dare you manhandle me in that way?' Mariah Beecham gasped her outrage at finding herself alone outside on the terrace with him.

'I believe you will find that I dare much in the protection of my impressionable younger brother, madam.' Darian looked down at her coldly. 'Most especially so when I have good reason to believe a woman such as yourself could never have any serious intentions with regard to a man as young and *inexperienced* as Anthony.'

'A woman such as me?' she repeated softly.

Darian nodded tersely. 'We must both be aware of your reputation, madam.'

She eyed him coldly. 'Must we?'

His gaze turned frosty at her tone. 'That reputation apart, you were married to a man at least twenty-five years your senior and now you are dallying with a man at least ten years younger than yourself.' Darian gave a shrug. 'Perhaps it is that you are afraid of entertaining the attentions of a man of your own age?'

Mariah knew that this man could have absolutely no idea of the unhappiness she had suffered during her years of marriage to the much older Martin Beecham; they had both taken great care, for their daughter, Christina's, sake, to ensure that society did not learn of their deep-felt dislike of each other.

As for her dallying with this man's younger brother? It was pure nonsense. The young Lord Anthony had certainly received no encouragement from her, in what Wolfingham now claimed was his brother's infatuation with her.

Truth be told, Mariah did not have a serious interest in any gentleman, her marriage to Martin having soured her towards spending too much time in the company of any man, let alone trusting her emotions, her heart, to one of them. In her opinion, all men were selfish and controlling. And she had no intentions of being controlled by anyone ever again.

Certainly not Wolfingham!

'A man such as yourself, you mean?' she taunted drily.

'I would appear to fit that criteria, yes,' he bit out harshly.

She gave a scornful smile. 'I believe you are still a year or two younger than I, Wolfingham. Nor, after this conversation, would I be foolish enough to ever believe any interest you showed in me, now or in the future, to be in the least sincere.'

Then she would be wrong, Darian acknowledged reluctantly. Because these past few minutes in her company had shown him he was very interested in Mariah Beecham. Intellectually as well as physically.

Not only was it an unwise interest on his part, but it was also a forbidden one, in light of Anthony's feelings for the woman. Darian could not be so disloyal to his brother as to try to win, and bed, the woman Anthony believed himself to be in love with.

'You would be perfectly correct to mistrust any such interest,' he conceded drily.

'Then if we have quite finished this conversation?' She arched haughty brows. 'It is rather chilly out here and I have other guests to attend to.'

'First I wish to know if it is your intention to continue seeing Anthony.'

'As it would appear he attends most, if not all, of the same entertainments as myself, I do not see how I can do otherwise.'

So much for his being a voice of reason, Darian derided himself impatiently. He seemed, in fact, to have only succeeded in making the situation worse, rather than better. By approaching Mariah Beecham and talking to her of his concern for Anthony, he appeared to have angered the lady into doing the opposite of what he asked.

Not only that, but he now seemed to have developed a physical desire for the woman himself!

She looked especially lovely in the moonlight, her hair having turned palest gold, her flawless skin pure ivory against the darker silk of her gown. As for her perfume! It was a mixture of flowers and some heady and exotic scent Darian could not quite place, but that seeped insidiously into his very pores, heightening his senses, so that he was aware only of the woman standing so proudly beautiful before him.

'Must we continue to argue about this, Mariah?' His voice lowered huskily even as he took a step forward.

Her gaze became guarded as she tilted her head further back in order to be able to look up at him. 'I have not given you permission to use my first name,' she bit out frostily. 'Nor am I aware of any argument between the two of us. You have made a request and I have discounted the very idea of there ever being any sort of alliance between your brother and myself. As far as I am concerned, that is an end to the subject.'

Darian drew in a deep breath. 'I do not see how it can be, when Anthony seems so set upon his pursuit of you.'

Mariah was not at all happy at the way Darian Hunter had moved so much closer to her. So close, in fact, that she felt as if her personal space had been invaded. And not in an altogether unpleasant way.

Her years of marriage to Martin had been extremely difficult ones, so much so that in the early years of their marriage she had preferred to remain secluded in the country. Maturity had brought with it a certain confidence, a knowledge, if you will, of her own powers as a woman, if not in regard to her husband, then at least towards the attentions shown to her by other gentlemen. With that confidence had come the art, the safety, of social flirtation, without the promise of there ever being anything more.

It was a veneer of sophistication that had stood her in good stead since Martin's death five years ago, when so many other gentlemen had decided that the now widowed and very wealthy Countess of Carlisle would make them an admirable wife.

As if Mariah would willingly forgo the newfound freedom and wealth that widowhood had given her, in order to become another man's wife and possession!

Oh, she knew well the reputation she had in society, of a woman who took as her lover any man she chose. Knew of it, because it was a reputation she had deliberately fostered; if Mariah Beecham was known only to take lovers, rather than having any intention of ever contemplating remarrying, then the fortune hunters, at least, were kept at bay.

Occasionally—as now!—a gentlemen would attempt to breach those walls she had placed about herself and her private life, but to date she had managed to thwart that interest without offence being taken on either side.

Even on such brief closer acquaintance, she knew that Darian Hunter, the powerful Duke of Wolfingham, was not a man to be gainsaid by flirtatious cajolery or, failing that, the cut direct.

And he was currently standing far too close to Mariah for her comfort.

'I have already told you that you must speak with your brother further on that subject, Wolfingham.' Mariah tilted her chin challengingly. 'Now if you would kindly step aside? As I have said, it is now my wish to return to my other guests.'

Instead of stepping away Darian took another step forward, at once assailed by the warmth of Mariah Beecham's closer proximity and the aroma of that exotic and unique perfume. 'And do you always get what you wish for, Mariah?' he prompted huskily.

The nerve fluttered, pulsed, in the slender length of her neck, as the only outward sign of her disquiet at his persistence. 'Rarely what I wish for,' she bit out tersely, 'but invariably what I want!'

'And what is it that you want now, I wonder?' Darian mused as he continued to breathe in, and be affected by, her heady perfume. 'Can it be that your air of uninterest and detachment is but a ruse? And that secretly, inwardly, you long for a man who will take the initiative, take control of the situation? To take control of you?'

'No!' the countess gasped, her face having paled in the moonlight.

His brow rose. 'Perhaps you protest too much?'

'I protest because it is how I genuinely feel,' she assured vehemently. 'I am no gentleman's plaything, to be controlled.'

'No?' One of Darian's hands moved up of its

own volition, with the intention of cupping the smooth curve of her cheek.

'Do not touch me!' She flinched back, her eyes huge turquoise pools now in the pallor of her face.

Darian frowned at her vehemence. 'But I should very much like to touch you, Mariah.'

'I *said*, do not touch me!' Her expression was one of grim determination as she reached up and attempted to physically push Darian away from her.

It was now Darian's turn to gasp, to lose his breath completely, as one of her tiny hands connected with his recently injured and painfully aching shoulder, causing pain such as he had never known before to burst, to course hotly, piercingly, through the whole length and breadth of his body.

He clasped his shoulder as he staggered back, his knees in danger of buckling beneath him at the depth of that pain, black spots appearing in front of his eyes even as his vision began to blur and darken.

'Wolfingham? Tell me what is wrong.'

Mariah Beecham's voice seemed to come from a long distance away as the darkness about Darian first thickened, then became absolute.

Chapter Two

Darian felt totally disorientated as the waves of darkness began to lift and he slowly awakened.

Quite *where* it was he had awakened to, he had no idea, as he turned from where he lay on the bed to look about the unfamiliar bedchamber.

It was most certainly a feminine room, decorated in pale lavenders and creams, with delicate white furnishings and lavender brocade curtains at the windows and about the four-poster bed on which he currently reclined, the pillows and bedclothes beneath him of pale lilac satin and lace.

It was Darian's idea of a feminine hell!

Certainly he felt ridiculous lying amongst such frills and fancies. Nor did he remember how he came to be here in the first place.

He recalled attending the Countess of Carlisle's

ball, dancing with her, and then that heated conversation with her on the terrace. Followed by the excruciating pain, and then—nothing. He remembered absolutely nothing of what had happened beyond that.

Either he was still at Mariah Beecham's home, which, considering their argument, he doubted very much, or he had gone on to a club or gaming hell, where he had drunk too much, before spending the night with some woman. Both would be uncharacteristic; Darian never drank too much when he was out and about in the evening, nor did he bed random women.

As such, neither of those explanations seemed likely for his current disorientation.

He struggled to sit up, with the intention of removing himself from his hellish surroundings. All to no avail, as he found it impossible to move his left arm.

Glancing down at the source of the problem, Darian realised that he was wearing only his pantaloons. His jacket, waistcoat, his shirt *and* his boots had all been removed and his left shoulder was now tightly strapped up in a white bandage, his arm immobilised in a sling across the bareness of his chest.

'And just what do you think you are doing?'

Darian, having finally managed to manoeuvre himself into a sitting position on the side of the bed, now turned sharply at the sound of that imperious voice, his eyes widening and then narrowing as Mariah Beecham stepped into the bedchamber and closed the door quietly behind her.

She was no longer dressed in the turquoise silk gown, but now wore a day-dress of sky blue, the style simpler, with just a touch of lace at the cap sleeves. Her hair was also less elaborately styled than at the ball, the blonde curls merely gathered up and secured at her crown and completely unadorned.

The reason for those changes in her appearance became apparent as she lightly crossed the room on slippered feet in order to pull back the lavender brocade curtains from across the windows, allowing the full light of day to shine into the bedchamber.

She turned to look across at him critically. 'You

are looking a little better this morning, Wolfing-ham. The doctor advised last night that you are *not* to attempt to get out of bed for several days,' she continued firmly as Darian would have stood up. 'You had burst several of the stitches on the wound on your shoulder and it was also in need of cleansing before new stitches and a bandage could be applied,' she added reprovingly.

Darian knew his wounded shoulder had been paining him for several days now, but at this moment it throbbed and ached like the very devil!

'Something, the doctor assured me yesterday evening as he reapplied those stitches, that you must have been aware of for some time before last night?' the countess added sternly.

Of course Darian had been aware of it, but his brother's future, and this unsuitable alliance, had been of more importance to him than his own painful shoulder. Nor was it the state of his own health that was now his main concern.

The reason for *that* was the how and why he came to still be in Mariah Beecham's home on the morning following her ball, for he had no choice but to accept that was where he was.

Darian frowned as he recalled their unsatis-
factory conversation on the terrace of Carlisle
House the evening before. How he had been unable to resist moving closer to Mariah, drawn by
her unique perfume and the temptation of the
perfection of her skin in the moonlight.

He also had a vague memory of Mariah reaching up to physically push him away after he had
ignored her instructions to step back from her.
The pain that had followed that push had been
excruciating. So intense that it had caused Darian's breath to cease and his knees to buckle as
the waves of blackness engulfed him. After that
he remembered nothing.

Did that mean he had remained unconscious
for the whole of the previous night?

That he had spent that night in Mariah Beecham's home? Possibly in her own bedchamber?

If that was indeed the case, then Darian certainly had no memory of any of those events.

But neither did he recall having departed Carlisle House. Or having been attended by a doctor.

'You are currently in one of my guest bedchambers,' the countess supplied drily, as his

horrified expression must have given away at least some of his thoughts. 'My daughter's choice rather than my own,' she continued with a rueful glance at their feminine surroundings.

Darian licked the dryness of his lips before speaking for the first time since he had awoken. 'Lady Christina knows I spent the night here?'

'Why, yes,' Mariah drawled, Wolfingham's obvious discomfort in his surroundings succeeding in dissipating some of her own irritation in having to accommodate him here for the night, following his faint the previous evening. 'There was nothing else to be done once you had fainted dead away on my terrace. What else would you have me call it, Wolfingham?' she added mockingly as he gave a grunt of protest.

He scowled his displeasure. 'I was obviously overcome with pain—to call it a faint makes me sound like a complete ninny.'

'It does rather.' She arched mocking brows. 'Very well, Wolfingham, when you were overcome with pain,' she conceded drily as he continued to glower. 'Whatever the cause, it left me with no choice but to have two of my footmen carry you up the servants' stairs, before placing you in one of the bedchambers and sending for the doctor—much as the temptation was for me to just leave you unconscious upon my terrace, apparently inebriated, for one of my other guests to find!' she added.

Green eyes narrowed. 'I suppose I should thank you for having resisted that particular temptation,' Wolfingham growled.

'I suppose you should, yes,' Mariah drawled dismissively. 'But I doubt you intend doing so?'

'Not at this moment, no,' Wolfingham bit out from between gritted teeth.

She gave a mocking shake of her head. 'Bad show, Wolfingham, when at considerable inconvenience to myself, I have undoubtedly helped you to maintain your reputation as being the stern and soberly respectable Duke of Wolfingham.'

His brow lowered darkly. 'You have also put me in the position of now having to remove myself from your home, without detection by a third party, on the morning following your ball.'

'And so tarnishing that sterling reputation anyway,' she derided. 'Poor Wolfingham!'

He remained disgruntled. 'My reputation in society is one of sternness and sober respectability?'

'Oh, yes.' Mariah strolled across to where Wolfingham still sat on the side of the bed, the darkness of his hair, tousled and unkempt, succeeding in lessening his usual air of austerity and also taking years off his age of two, or possibly three, and thirty.

Nevertheless, it was far safer for Mariah to take in the tousled appearance of Wolfingham's hair than to allow her gaze to move any lower. To where the removal of his top clothes had rendered Darian Hunter naked from the waist up, apart from the bandage and sling the doctor had placed about his left shoulder and arm the night before.

And a very masculine and muscled chest it was, too, with a light dusting of dark hair, which deepened to a vee down the firm and muscled length of his stomach, before disappearing into the loosened waistband of his black evening trousers.

None of which Mariah was at all happy to

realise she had taken note of! 'The doctor remarked that the original injury to your shoulder has all the appearance of being a bullet wound,' she said challengingly. 'And was possibly inflicted a week or so ago?'

'Six days ago, to be precise,' he conceded gruffly. 'I would now have your word that you will not discuss this with anyone else,' he added harshly.

Her eyebrows rose. 'And will you trust my word if it is given?'

'I will.' Darian had little choice in the matter but to trust to Mariah Beecham's discretion. Besides which, there might be plenty of gossip in society in regard to the countess, but he had never heard of her having discussed with anyone the gentlemen with whom she was known to have been intimately involved.

'Then you have it.' She nodded now. 'Nevertheless, I should be interested to learn how you came to receive such a wound. Unless England is already once again at war and I am unaware of it?' She arched mocking blonde brows.

Darian knew that for most women, this would

have been her first question upon entering the bedchamber and finding her uninvited guest had finally awoken from his stupor!

But, as he had learnt yesterday evening, Mariah Beecham was not like most women. Indeed, he truly had no idea what manner of woman she was. Which only added to her mystique.

And attraction?

Yesterday evening Mariah Beecham had given the appearance of being the sophisticated and confident woman of society that she undoubtedly was. Today, free of adornment or artifice, Mariah Beecham looked no older than her seventeen-year-old daughter.

Her figure was that of a mature woman, of course, but her face was smooth and unlined in the sunlight, her eyes a clear Mediterranean turquoise, despite her having hosted a ball the previous evening and no doubt having retired very late to her own bedchamber.

Darian felt that stirring of his arousal, which was rapidly becoming a familiar reaction to being in this woman's company, as he gazed upon her natural loveliness through narrowed lids. 'I fear that peace will not last for too much longer, now that Napoleon has returned to France and is currently reported to be on his way to Paris,' he rasped in an attempt to dampen his physical response to this woman.

'I do not interest myself in such boring things as politics and intrigue,' she drawled dismissively. 'Nor does any of that explain how you came to receive such a wound.' She continued to look at him pointedly, before a derisive smile slowly curved the fullness of her lips at his continued silence. 'Can it be that the cold and haughty Duke of Wolfingham has recently fought a duel? Over a woman? Surely not?' Mocking humour now gleamed in her eyes.

Darian had not cared for the disparaging way in which Mariah Beecham had earlier said his reputation was one of sober respectability. Or that she now referred to him as the cold and haughty Duke of Wolfingham. Nor did Darian like the implication that she doubted he had ever felt so emotional about any woman that he would have fought a duel over her.

Admittedly, he was, by nature, a private man.

One who had long preferred his own company or that of his few close friends. But he'd had no idea, until now, that this privacy of nature had resulted in society, in Mariah Beecham, believing him to be sober—boring?—as well as cold and haughty—arrogant?

As the elder son of the sixth Duke of Wolfingham, and Marquis of Durham from birth, Darian had been brought up to know he would one day inherit the title of Duke from his father, along with the management of all the estates entailed with the title. An onerous and unenviable responsibility, which had become his at the age of only five and twenty; much earlier than might have been expected, but his father had been but sixty years of age when he died.

With the title of Duke and its other onerous responsibilities had also come the guardianship of his younger brother, Anthony.

All of these things had made it impossible for Darian to continue with the hedonistic pursuits he had previously enjoyed with his close friends and that, along with his soldiering, had hitherto occupied much of his time.

He had not realised until now that it had also rendered him as being thought stern and sober, as well as haughty. By society as a whole, it would appear, and by this woman in particular.

Nor did he care to be thought so now, for it made him sound as old as Methuselah and just as uninteresting! A circumstance Darian did not enjoy, when he considered his own undoubted physical response to Mariah Beecham.

His mouth tightened. 'I am sure you are as aware as I that the fighting of duels is forbidden.'

She arched blonde brows. 'And do you always follow the rules, Wolfingham?'

Darian gave a humourless smile. 'Your opinion of my reputation would seem to imply as much.'

'But we are all so much more than our reputations, are we not?' Mariah Beecham replied enigmatically.

'Do you include yourself in that statement?' Darian studied her through narrowed lids, taking note of that curling golden hair, the smoothness of her brow, those clear and untroubled blue eyes and the light blush that now coloured her alabaster cheeks, her lips both full and succulent.

A face that appeared utterly without guilt or guile.

Misleadingly so? Or could that air of innocence, so unusual in a woman of four and thirty, possibly be the real Mariah Beecham?

In view of this woman's reputation, Darian found that impossible to believe; the countess could no doubt add 'accomplished actress' to her list of other questionable attributes!

Mariah did not at all care for the way in which Wolfingham was now studying her so intently.

Having Wolfingham point out, the previous evening, that his younger brother had shown a marked interest in her these past weeks was irritating enough. But to have the far too astute, and equally as intelligent, Darian Hunter, the Duke of Wolfingham, show an interest in her, for whatever reason, was not only disturbing, but could also be dangerous.

For Mariah was most certainly not all that her reputation implied. Indeed, she did not believe, after Wolfingham's revelations the night before regarding that reputation, that she was much of any of what society, or this man, believed her to be.

Deliberately so. For who would suspect that the scandalous Mariah Beecham, the widowed Countess of Carlisle, was also an agent for the Crown, and that she had been so these past seven years and more?

She had not set out for it to be so. She had become embroiled in the intrigues of the English court quite by accident, after discovering that her own husband was a traitor to both his country and his king.

Having no idea what to do with that knowledge, it had taken Mariah some weeks to find a member of the government to whom she might pass along that information.

Only to discover that once she had done so the first time, there was no going back. That her position in society could, and did, open many doors, as it invited confidences from both ladies and gentlemen of the *ton.*

And so, from that time on Mariah had made a point of forming her friendships only with those ladies and gentlemen who might have knowledge that would be of benefit to, or was opposed to, the English monarchy or government.

She had been brought up in the knowledge that her parents' only expectation of her was that she become the wife of a titled gentleman, even if she did not love that gentleman. Her father was himself extremely wealthy, but not completely acceptable to all of society. Indeed, greater acquaintance with society had shown her that love was not a requirement of any of the *ton*'s marriages.

Her husband's only expectation of her had been that she bring a considerable portion of her father's fortune to their marriage, his own fortune having become depleted almost to extinction.

Mariah loved her daughter dearly and, because of that, had willingly sacrificed the years she had suffered of being thought of as just an adjunct of her husband, Lord Martin Beecham, the Earl of Carlisle.

Finding herself suddenly of use, her opinions of importance, had caused Mariah to relish the new role in her life.

As a consequence, the past seven years were

the first ones where Mariah had felt useful and valued for herself alone.

She would be unable to continue along that path if anyone in society were to ever discover that she used her title and wealth only as a way in which she might work, and spy, for the Crown.

If the shrewd Darian Hunter, Duke of Wolfingham, were to ever discover her work as a spy for the Crown…

She forced a teasing smile to now curve her lips. 'Surely that is for me to know and for others to find out?'

Darian drew in a sharp breath at Mariah Beecham's huskily flirtatious tone, a quiver of awareness tingling down the length of his spine as his body responded.

At the same time, he sensed that Mariah's flirtation was somehow not genuine, but forced, although he had no idea why that should be.

Indeed, nothing about this woman, or her actions, was in the least clear to him. And until such time as it was, if it ever was, he would be well advised to remain wary in her company.

'Considering that you have refused my request

to discourage my brother's interest in you,' he answered her briskly as he stood up, 'and the amount of times our paths have chanced to cross these past seven years or more, I very much doubt there will be any opportunity in future for me to know you any better than I do at this moment.'

'Do I detect a note of regret in your tone?' she taunted.

'Not in the least,' Darian dismissed harshly. 'I am more than ready to leave and so end our acquaintance.'

'Then you had best do so,' she drawled unconcernedly.

His eyes narrowed. 'Did you dismiss my carriage last night?'

The countess laughed huskily. 'Tempted as I was to do otherwise!' She nodded in confirmation. 'It might have been amusing to see how you would have explained that occurrence to any who cared to ask. But, of course, you are Wolfingham, one of The Dangerous Dukes,' she continued drily. 'And like your four friends, Wolfingham does not care to explain himself, to any man or woman!'

Darian's eyes narrowed. 'You do not have a very good opinion of me, do you?'

'Until yesterday evening I do not believe I held any opinion of you whatsoever,' she assured uninterestedly.

His breath caught in his throat at that dismissal; if he did not care to explain himself to man or woman then it was equally as true that same man or woman would never dare to question him, either! 'And now?'

'Now I know without a doubt that you are both arrogant and insulting.'

Darian winced at her dismissive tone, knowing that he had been both of those things in his dealings with this woman. 'If you would kindly send word to Wolfingham House, via one of your obviously capable footmen, and inform my butler that I have need of my carriage, I will then be able to remove my intrusive self from both your household and your presence!'

Mariah felt a sense of disquiet at the abruptness of Wolfingham's departure. 'I had not expected you to capitulate quite so easily, Wolfingham, in regard to my continuing friendship with your brother?' she mocked.

'I am not capitulating, merely withdrawing in order to rethink my strategy,' he assured drily.

'Ah.' Mariah nodded knowingly. 'I remind you that the doctor instructed that you were to remain abed for the next three days at least.'

Having now crossed to where his clothes lay draped over the bedroom chair, Wolfingham turned to look at her with those narrowed green eyes.

Green eyes surrounded by the longest, thickest, darkest lashes Mariah had seen on any man.

Indeed, Darian Hunter was a man of startling and masculine good looks; the nakedness of his back was exceedingly broad and muscled for a man who supposedly ran his estates from the comfort of his home here in London. As were his arms and the flatness of his abdomen, his legs also appearing long and muscled in those black evening trousers. Even his feet, *sans* his boots, bore a long and elegant appearance.

And Mariah could not remember the last time

she had noticed the masculine beauty of any man, fully clothed or otherwise!

Perhaps when she had been Christina's age, and on the brink of womanhood, she might have allowed her head to be turned a time or two by a handsome gentleman, but certainly not at any time since. The very nature of her marriage to Martin Beecham had meant there had never been any further inclination on her part to indulge in those girlish infatuations.

But Mariah could not deny, to herself at least, that she had noticed, and been aware of, every muscle and sinew of Darian Hunter's muscular torso these past few minutes. And also been affected by it, as the slight fluttering of her pulse, the warmth in her cheeks and the aching fullness of her breasts all testified.

And she did not want to feel any of those things for any man!

Warning her that Darian Hunter more than lived up to his dangerous reputation, not only to her continued work for the Crown, but also to Mariah's own peace of mind.

'Nor shall I once I am returned to it,' Darian

now answered the countess huskily, aware of the sudden, sexual, tension in the heavy still-ness of the bedchamber. 'As for my brother, if all else fails, then I fear Anthony must learn of the vagaries of women in the way that all men do—the hard way!' he added derisively.

'Now you are being deliberately insult-ing again, Wolfingham, not just to me, but all women.' An angry flush now coloured Mariah Beecham's cheeks.

A blush that only succeeded in enhancing her beauty; her eyes glittered that deep turquoise, her cheeks glowing, her lips having become a deep and rosy red.

A very kissable deep and rosy red...

'That was not my intention,' Darian dismissed softly.

'No?'

'I believe my remark was more specific than that,' he assured huskily, holding Mariah's gaze as he slowly crossed to where she stood so stiff and challenging in the middle of the bedcham-ber. 'Might I ask for your assistance in dressing? I realise it is usual for a man to ask a woman for help to *un*dress,' he added drily as Mariah's brows rose in obvious surprise at his request, 'but I am unable to pull my shirt on over my head on my own.'

Mariah accepted that Wolfingham's request for assistance was perfectly logical, given his injury, and yet she still baulked at the thought of performing such a task of intimacy for him.

She very much doubted that Wolfingham— or any in society!—would believe it if told, but Mariah had seen no man, other than her husband, even half-naked as Wolfingham now was. And Martin, twenty-five years her senior, had certainly never possessed the same muscular and disturbing physique Wolfingham now displayed so splendidly.

Her mouth firmed. 'I will send for one of my footmen to assist you.'

'There is no need for that, surely, when you are standing right here before me?' Darian murmured throatily, his good sense having once again deserted him as he was again assaulted by Mariah Beecham's unique and arousing perfume. An arousal he was finding it more and more difficult to control when in this woman's presence.

In view of Anthony's infatuation with Mariah Beecham, it would be unwise for Darian to allow his own attraction to her to develop into anything deeper than the physical discomfort it already was. Even if Mariah Beecham was herself agreeable to taking it any further, which he already knew that she was not.

On a logical level, Darian knew and accepted all of those things.

Unfortunately, his aroused and hardened body had a completely different opinion on the matter!

'If you please?' His gaze was intent upon her face now as he held out his shirt to her, allowing him to note the deepening of the blush that coloured her cheeks and the pulse throbbing at the base of her slender throat.

A surprising physical reaction, surely, coming from an experienced woman reputed to have indulged in many affairs, both during her marriage and since?

Darian's gaze narrowed searchingly as she stubbornly lifted her chin to meet his challenging gaze. She still made no effort to relieve him of his shirt. 'Unless, of course, you find the idea, and me, too repulsive...?'

It took every effort of Mariah's will to hold back the choked, slightly hysterical, laugh that threatened to burst from her throat, at the mere suggestion that any woman, that *she*, might find anything about Wolfingham in the least repulsive.

For the first time, in more years than she cared to remember, Mariah found herself wholly and completely physically aware of a man.

Of Darian Hunter, the arrogant and contemptuous Duke of Wolfingham, of all men.

Nevertheless, Mariah was aware. Of his reassuring height. His rakishly handsome good looks. And the lean and muscled strength of his body.

And she did not welcome the sensation.

She placed a disdainful curl on her lips. 'It is certainly true that I have always been...particular...as to which men I choose to be intimate with.'

'All evidence to the contrary, madam!'

Mariah drew her breath in sharply at the unexpected and contemptuously delivered insult,
before just as quickly masking that response;
the sophisticated and experienced Mariah Beecham—a public persona she had deliberately
nurtured these past seven years—would laugh
derisively in the face of such an insult.

Which was exactly what Mariah did now. 'I
am flattered that you should have even taken the
time to notice such things in regard to myself,
Wolfingham.'

His nostrils flared. 'You take delight in your
reputation?'

Did she?

Oh, yes!

It was Mariah's own personal joke on society,
that they should all perceive her as being one
thing and she knew herself to be something else
entirely. Only her darling Christina, now seventeen, and currently enjoying her very first Season, had necessarily been informed of the true
reason for Mariah's flirtatious behaviour in public. It was a risk to share that confidence with
anyone, of course, but Mariah simply could not

have borne for her darling daughter, the person she loved most in all the world, to ever believe the nonsense society gossiped about her.

'No doubt as much as you do your own,' Mariah now dismissed enigmatically.

Darian scowled as he recalled what this woman had described as being his reputation. 'Then that would be not at all.'

She smiled. 'Unfortunately, even you cannot dictate what society thinks of you.'

'Even I?'

'Why, yes, for you are the omnipotent Duke of Wolfingham, are you not?' she dismissed airily. 'Your shirt, if you please,' she instructed briskly, reaching out to take the item of clothing from him. Wolfingham continued to hold on to it, standing far too close to her while he did so.

Darian looked down at her intently, wishing he knew at least some of the thoughts going on inside that surprisingly intelligent head of hers. Before speaking with Mariah Beecham yesterday evening, Darian would have described her, had considered her, as nothing more than an empty-headed flirt, with little in her beautiful head but the pursuit of her own pleasure.

He still had no idea of what or who Mariah Beecham truly was, but an empty-headed flirt she certainly was not.

Rendering her flirtation with Anthony, a man fully ten years her junior, all the more puzzling.

'Mariah—' Darian broke off his husky query as there was the briefest of knocks on the door to the bedchamber before it was opened.

'Mama, I—' Lady Christina Beecham stopped what she had been about to say as she stood in the open doorway, eyes wide as she took in the apparent cameo of intimacy between her mother and their half-dressed guest.

Darian had certainly never been discovered in quite such a scene of apparent intimacy by the daughter of any woman, and he now found himself momentarily nonplussed as he searched his mind for something appropriate to say or do. He frowned down at Mariah Beecham as she looked up at him. She began to chuckle huskily, before that chuckle became a full-throated laugh of pure enjoyment.

At Darian's obvious expense…

Chapter Three

'I trust, Lady Christina, that you do not think too badly of me for the circumstances under which we last met?' Darian murmured politely as the two of them danced together at Lady Stockton's ball, fully a week after their first momentous meeting in a guest bedchamber at Carlisle House.

A week in which Darian had necessarily to spend most of his time in his own bed, recovering from the setback from his bullet wound. For much of that time he'd found his thoughts returning to that morning in Mariah Beecham's guest bedchamber.

Not that there had been a great deal for him to remember and think about once Christina Beecham had appeared in the bedchamber so unexpectedly.

Mariah's amusement at the interruption had been short-lived, her movements having then become brisk and businesslike as she had helped Darian on with his shirt before excusing herself to go downstairs and see to the ordering of his carriage. The two ladies had left the bedchamber arm in arm together.

Darian had felt surprisingly weak after having completed dressing himself as best he could, sitting on the side of the bed to recover as he awaited the arrival of his carriage. Once arrived, his groom had then helped him down the stairs and into that carriage, necessitating that Darian's words of gratitude for the countess's assistance be brief.

Once returned to Wolfingham House, he had sent for his own physician, who'd agreed with his colleague's diagnosis, as he confined Darian to bed for the next three days at least, and rest thereafter for several more days, unless Darian wished to shuffle off his mortal coil completely.

Darian despised any form of weakness, in himself more than others, and that enforced time abed had not sat easily upon his shoulders, despite receiving several visits from his closest friends to help relieve the boredom. Anthony had also called upon him several times and been told that Darian was indisposed and not receiving visitors, which allowed Darian to at least avoid that particular confrontation until he was feeling more himself.

He had to trust that the countess would keep her promise in regard to discussing with others the bullet wound to his shoulder and the night he had necessarily spent in her home. But he had no doubt Mariah would have taken great delight in regaling Anthony with the details of Darian's efforts to persuade her to end their friendship.

Once he felt well enough, Darian had dictated a letter of gratitude to his secretary, to be delivered to the countess, carefully worded so as not to reveal the full extent of his indebtedness to her. He had received no acknowledgement or reply to that missive. As if Mariah Beecham, like himself, would prefer to continue as if that night had not taken place at all.

Consequently, this was the first occasion upon which Darian had been able to offer his apologies in person, to the younger of the two Beecham ladies at least, for the manner of his indisposition the week before.

Mariah Beecham had proved somewhat more elusive this evening than her daughter, always flirting or dancing away on the arm of some other gentleman whenever Darian had attempted to approach her. Christina Beecham had proved far less averse to his request that she dance a set with him. No doubt, unlike her mother before her, Christina Beecham was fully aware of the compliment being paid to her, as the Duke of Wolfingham did not, as a rule, dance at any of these occasions.

She looked up at him shyly now from between thick blonde lashes, her eyes the same beautiful turquoise colour as her mother's, her blonde-haired beauty also similar to that of the countess. 'Mama has already explained the situation to me, your Grace,' she now dismissed huskily.

Darian would be very interested to hear how Mariah had managed to do that, when he was not altogether sure how to explain the situation himself. *To* himself, as well as to others.

'Indeed,' he murmured noncommittally. 'She seems to be fully occupied this evening.' Another glance about the ballroom had shown him that Mariah Beecham was no longer in the room.

Christina gave a smile of affection. 'Mama's time, and dance card, are always fully occupied at such entertainments as these, your Grace.'

Darian looked down searchingly at the younger of the Beecham ladies. 'And are you not bothered by having to witness the spectacle of seeing so many gentlemen flirting and leering at your mother's— Forgive me,' he bit out stiffly. 'That was unforgivably rude of me.' And, he realised, far too close to his feelings on the matter for his own comfort.

Mariah was wearing a red silk gown this evening, with a very low *décolletage* that revealed the full, ivory swell of the tops of her breasts. A fact Darian had noted several gentlemen taking advantage of as they talked or danced with her.

'Yes, it was,' Christina Beecham answered him with the same bluntness as her mother. 'But then, Mama had already warned me you are very forthright, in both your manner and speech,' she added pertly.

Darian found he did not care for being dismissed so scathingly. Nor did he believe Mariah had used a word so innocent as 'forthright' to describe his previous manner and conversations with her. 'I meant no disrespect to you,' he bit out tersely.

'Only to Mama,' she acknowledged drily. 'Mama has taught me that it is better not to pass comment on what one does not know.'

'Obviously my own mother was neglectful in that particular duty.'

'Obviously.'

Yes, this lady, for all she was very young, was proving to be just as capable of delivering a set-down as her mother!

Darian was also aware that his own reaction to those flirting and leering gentlemen was not one of impartiality, but rather one of complete partiality. Indeed, he had disliked intensely to have to stand by and witness those other gentlemen showing Mariah such marked attentions.

In truth, he had thought of Mariah Beecham far more than was wise this past week. Of her beauty. Her unique perfume. Of his own physical and uncontrollable response to the lush curves of her body.

And, quite frankly, he found the whole situation annoying. Distracting. *Unbearable.*

'My dance, I believe, Darian?'

Darian roused himself from those troubling thoughts to look about him almost dazedly; the music had stopped playing and the other couples had left the dance floor, as they now gave curious glances their way. All without Darian having been aware of any of it. His brother, Anthony, was also now standing beside him with eyebrows raised expectantly, as he waited for Darian to release Christina Beecham.

'Of course.' He straightened abruptly as his arms fell back to his sides and he stepped away from Lady Christina. 'I— Thank you,' he added with a belated bow towards the young lady.

Anthony continued to look at him frowningly, eyes narrowed speculatively as he took his brother's place at Christina Beecham's side. 'Are you quite well again now, Darian?'

'Quite, thank you.' Darian nodded abruptly.

'In that case I will call upon you tomorrow,' Anthony stated firmly, his expression challenging, telling Darian that the conversation between the two of them might have been delayed for this past week, whilst he was feeling unwell, but it was not to be avoided altogether!

'Very well.' Darian gave another distracted nod as he once again glanced about the ballroom to see that the three of them were still the focus of more than one group of gossiping people.

'Your Grace?'

'Lady Christina?' Darian turned, one brow raised enquiringly.

A sparkle of humour now brightened those eyes, so like her mother's. 'I believe Mama to have accepted Lord Maystone's invitation to accompany him into the next room to partake of refreshment.'

Had he made his interest in Mariah's whereabouts so obvious that even her daughter was aware of it?

And what the deuce was Mariah doing in Maystone's company, a gentleman Darian had reason to know rather better than might be socially apparent?

Aged in his late fifties, and a widower for more than twenty years, Aubrey Maystone was nevertheless still a handsome man, with his head of silver hair and chiselled features. Nor had his trimness gone to obesity, as had happened to so many of his peers.

He was also Darian's contact at the Foreign Office in regard to his work for the Crown.

Whatever the reason for Aubrey Maystone's interest in Mariah, Darian had no intentions of wasting any more of his own time this evening in an effort to secure the opportunity in which to converse with her again.

He took care to avoid his brother's no-doubt accusing gaze as he gave Lady Christina a rueful smile. 'Thank you.' He gave another bow before turning to cross the ballroom in long and determined strides as he went in search of the refreshment room.

And Mariah Beecham.

* * *

'I believe you have accepted an invitation to attend Lord and Lady Nicholses' house party in Kent this weekend?' Lord Maystone nodded his acquaintance to Mrs Moore, as she stood across the room, even as he continued his softly spoken conversation with Mariah.

'I have, yes.' Mariah eyed him curiously. 'Will you also be attending?'

'Good heavens, no!' Maystone turned to give her his full attention, a look of distaste upon his lined but handsome face. 'Subjecting myself to a single tedious evening of socialising in a week is quite enough for me. I assure you, I have no intentions of suffering through a weekend of it.'

'Poor Aubrey.' Mariah chuckled sympathetically, placing a conciliatory hand briefly on his arm as she sobered. 'Do you have a special reason for asking whether or not I am to attend this particular weekend party?' Aubrey Maystone had long been her contact for the work she did for the Crown.

'I have reason to believe— Ah, Wolfingham.' Aubrey turned to greet the younger man warmly.

'Just the man! The countess is as polite as she is beautiful, but nevertheless I believe her to be in need of far younger company than my own.'

Mariah was relieved she had her back turned towards Darian Hunter, so he would not mistake the colour in her cheeks for anything other than what it was: annoyance at the way in which he had seemed to dog her every step this evening.

Lady Stockton had obviously been as surprised as her guests when the Duke of Wolfingham, a man who rarely attended any of the entertainments of the *ton*, but who had now attended two in as many weeks, had arrived at her home earlier this evening. A surprise that had lasted for only a few seconds, as that lady hastily crossed the room to welcome her illustrious guest.

Mariah's reaction to seeing Wolfingham again had been less enthusiastic. She wondered what he was doing here.

Indeed, she had gone out of her way not to show any reaction at all, but rather to ignore him completely.

Not an easy task, when it seemed that every time she had turned round this evening Wolfingham had been standing there behind her, looking very dark and handsome in his impeccable evening clothes, the darkness of his hair rakishly dishevelled.

Nor did Mariah believe his appearance now, in the refreshment room, to be coincidental, either.

No doubt, whilst forced to convalesce, in order to recover completely from his injury, the duke had also had time to rethink his decision not to leave his younger brother's fate to chance—or Mariah's caprice or whimsy.

Whatever the reasoning behind Wolfingham's dogged persistence this evening, Mariah was more than a little weary of reassuring him that she had absolutely no romantic interest, nor would she ever have, in his brother, Anthony.

'Not at all, Aubrey.' She gave Maystone a warm smile as she now linked her arm with his. 'Indeed, you are so handsome and distinguished that you put all younger men to shame,' she added before turning to look up at Wolfingham now that she felt reassured her cheeks were no longer flushed.

Darian's lips twitched and he held back a smile

as he met Mariah Beecham's challenging gaze, recognising her remark for exactly what it was: an insult to him rather than just a compliment to Aubrey Maystone.

Although the warmth of familiarity between the two of them did seem to imply a deeper acquaintance than just a socially polite one.

To the degree that Maystone might be Mariah's current lover? If that was so, then it made a nonsense of Darian's request that she cease her friendship with the far more youthful and inexperienced Anthony.

The possibility of that being true also brought a scowl to Darian's brow. 'Lady Beecham.' He bowed formally as it was the first occasion upon which the two of them had actually spoken this evening; Mariah's avoidance of him had been absolute. 'Maystone.' Darian's nod to the older man was terse.

'Wolfingham.' There was a mischievous twinkle in the older man's eyes, as if he had guessed Darian's thoughts and was amused by them. 'Have you come to steal Mariah away from me for a dance, or are you going to join us in some refreshment?'

'Well, I am certainly not here for refreshment.' Darian made no effort to hide his distaste as he eyed the glasses in their hands. 'I have heard it said that Lady Stockton is parsimonious with the brandy in her punch.'

'Surely it is not necessary to become inebriated in order to enjoy oneself?' Mariah drawled mockingly.

'Not at all.' Darian observed her between narrowed lids. 'But if I wished to drink something as innocuous as fruit juice then I should request fruit juice.' Standing so close to Mariah, he was once again aware of her unique perfume, the lightness of spring flowers and that deeper, more exotic perfume, which he now recognised as being jasmine. It was a heady and arousing combination.

'How true.' Maystone's dismissive laugh broke the tension that had been steadily rising between Darian and Mariah. 'It seems I must forgo your delightful company for now, my dear.' He placed his glass down on the table and raised Mariah's gloved hand to his lips before releasing it. 'And allow a younger man to steal you away from me for a dance.'

Mariah frowned as she answered coolly, 'To my knowledge, his Grace has not had the foresight to request a dance with me this evening. As such, I am afraid my dance card is completely full.'

'Well, there you have it, Wolfingham.' Maystone turned towards him with a grin. 'You will have to be much quicker off the mark in future, if you are to secure a dance with our delightful Mariah,' he teased jovially.

Darian's frustration with his own increasing arousal, as well as Mariah's avoidance of him, was now such that he could barely keep the impatience from his tone and he knew the frown had deepened on his brow. 'A pity, of course, Lady Beecham,' he drawled coldly. 'But as consolation I have just enjoyed the pleasure of dancing with your lovely daughter, Lady Christina. A delightful young woman and a credit to both you and her father.'

Mariah looked up sharply at Wolfingham,

easily noting the mocking challenge in his deep green eyes as he returned her gaze unblinkingly. No doubt because he was fully aware of the fact that she would prefer that he stay well away from her young and impressionable daughter.

Oh, Christina had accepted readily enough Mariah's explanations as to Wolfingham's indisposition the previous week having been the reason for his having to remain at Carlisle House overnight. But beneath that acceptance there had been an underlying girlish excitement, a curiosity, about the arrogantly handsome and illustrious Duke of Wolfingham. The last thing Mariah wished was for Christina to develop a crush on the man.

Not that she thought Wolfingham was in the least serious in his attentions to Christina; rather Mariah believed his intention had merely been to annoy her. If so, he had succeeded!

The less she, and Christina, had to do with Darian Hunter, the dangerous Duke of Wolfingham, the better Mariah would like it. Her lifestyle was such, most especially her work for the Crown, that she did not wish to have such an astutely disturbing gentleman as Wolfingham taking an interest in it, or her.

'I believe the music and dancing have now stopped for supper, your Grace.' Mariah had noted the influx of people into the room and strolling towards the supper tables. 'It appears to be raining outside, so perhaps you might care to accompany me for a stroll in the West Gallery?' At which time she intended to warn him to stay away from her daughter!

Darian was not particularly proud of himself for having used Lady Christina Beecham as a means of securing Mariah's company, but neither was he about to apologise for it. Not when it had succeeded in accomplishing his aim, which was to talk with Mariah again. In private.

Although he wasn't sure that being alone with Mariah was an entirely good idea, given his painful state of arousal.

'You will stay away from my daughter!' Mariah barely waited until the two of them had entered the long and deserted picture gallery, lit by a dozen candles or more, before removing her hand from Wolfingham's arm and glaring up at him, her cheeks hot with temper in the candlelight.

'Will I?' he came back with infuriating calm, dark brows raised in equally as mild query.

'Yes—when it is not a serious interest, but merely a means of punishing me.'

'That is not very flattering to Lady Christina.'

'But true.'

'Is it?' he returned mildly.

'What do you want from me, Wolfingham?' Mariah looked up at him in exasperation. 'A public declaration of my uninterest in your brother? Would that appease you? Reassure you?'

He gave a humourless smile. 'It would most certainly not appease or reassure Anthony.' His mouth tightened. 'Nor would it do anything for my own future relationship with him, if you were to tell him that I had been instrumental in bringing about the sudden end to your friendship.'

Mariah drew in a deep breath through her nose. 'Perhaps you should have thought of that before you chose to so arrogantly interfere in his life a week ago?'

'What is your relationship with Maystone?'

Mariah was momentarily disconcerted by this sudden change of topic. As she was meant to be?

She and Aubrey Maystone preferred to keep the true nature of their relationship private and as such it was rare for them to pass any time together in public. Indeed, they would not have done so this evening if Aubrey had not expressed a wish to speak with her urgently. A conversation that had been cut short by the arrival of Darian Hunter.

But the manner of the public acquaintance between Mariah and Lord Maystone was such that Wolfingham could not possibly have guessed that there was a deeper, more private, connection between the two of them. Could he?

Mariah was quickly learning that it would not be wise on her part, or anyone else's, to underestimate the intelligence or astuteness of Darian Hunter.

'My acquaintance with Lord Maystone is a long-standing one,' she answered frostily. 'Come about because he was once a friend of my late husband.'

'And is that all he is to you?'

'What are you accusing me of now, Wolfingham?' Her tone was impatiently exasperated, deliberately so. 'Do you imagine that I am currently enjoying a relationship with Lord Maystone, as well as your brother? Would that not make my bed very overcrowded?' she added scathingly. 'And what business would it be of yours, even if that were the case? I am a widow and they are both unattached gentlemen, so there is no prior claim to hinder the existence of either relationship.' She gave a dismissive shrug.

A nerve pulsed in the duke's tightly clenched jaw. 'Except a moral one.'

'You are a fine one to preach to me of morals, Wolfingham, when you are currently sporting the bullet wound you received whilst fighting a duel over some woman!' Her eyes flashed in the candlelight.

Darian glowered his frustration down at her, wanting to deny the accusation, but knowing that to do so would then bring the real cause of that wound back into question. A question he would not, could not, answer.

Having no answer, he decided to act instead.

Although that was possibly an exaggeration on his part, when his arms seemed to have moved of their own volition as they encircled Mariah's waist and he pulled her in close against the hardness of his body.

Her exotic perfume immediately filled all of his senses as his head swooped down to capture her lips with his own. Soft and delectable lips that had parted with surprise, so allowing for further intimacy as Darian's tongue swept lightly across her lips before plunging into the heated warmth beneath.

She felt so slender in his arms, the fullness of her breasts crushed against his chest, her lips and mouth tasting of honey. A silky-soft sweetness and heat that drew Darian in even closer, as he attempted to claim, to possess, that heat as his own. To claim, to possess, Mariah as his own.

Mariah had been totally unprepared for Wolfingham taking her into his arms, let alone having him kiss her. So unprepared, that for several stunned seconds she found herself responding to that kiss as her hands moved up to cling to the lapels of the duke's evening coat, her body crushed, aligned with Wolfingham's, as his mouth continued to plunder and claim her own. Making her fully aware not only of the hardness of his chest, but also the long length of his arousal pressing against the warmth of her abdomen.

She allowed herself to feel a brief moment of triumph, at the knowledge, this physical evidence, that Darian Hunter, the coldly arrogant Duke of Wolfingham, was aroused by her. From holding her in his arms. From kissing her.

Those brief moments of triumph were quickly followed by ones of panic and a desperate need to free herself. A move she attempted to instigate as she now pushed against that hard and muscled chest even as she wrenched her mouth out from beneath that sensually punishing kiss. 'Release me immediately, Wolfingham!'

Her eyes now gleamed up at him in the candlelight, her chest quickly rising and falling as she breathed heavily, having managed to put several inches between the hardness of his body and her own, but failing to release herself completely.

'You are taking your protection of your brother

too far, sir,' she added fiercely as her hands against his chest kept him at a distance but he still made no effort to remove the steel band of his arms from about her waist.

A nerve pulsed in the tightness of his jaw. 'This has nothing to do with my brother.'

'It has everything to do with him.'

Darian was breathing heavily, unable to reason clearly as he looked down at Mariah, his mind and senses too full of her to form a coherent thought, other than the taste of her on his own lips and tongue. The feel of her soft curves against his much harder ones. The smell of her causing his body to throb and pound with need.

A need that the pallor of Mariah's face in the candlelight, and over-bright turquoise eyes, said she did not reciprocate.

He gave a pained frown. 'What did you think would happen when you invited me to join you alone here in the gallery, Mariah?'

'Not this!' Her breasts quickly rose and fell in rhythm with her agitated breathing as she continued to hold him at arm's length. 'Never this!'

Darian's frown deepened to one of concern

as he heard the underlying sob in her voice. 'Mariah—'

'I believe the lady has expressed a wish to be set free, Darian!'

Darian's head whipped round at the sound of his brother's harshly reproving voice, a scowl darkening his brow as he saw Anthony watching them from the shadowed doorway into the gallery, the expression on his brother's face one of disgust as well as fury.

A disgust and fury Darian fully deserved, given the circumstances, of Mariah's obvious distress and the feelings Anthony had previously expressed for the woman Darian now held in his arms.

Feelings that Darian had totally forgotten about in his need to claim Mariah's lips for his own.

His arms fell heavily back to his sides as he stepped back and away from her, only to then reach out a hand to steady Mariah as she appeared to stumble.

'Do not touch me!' she lashed out verbally even as she pulled free of his grasp, twin spots of fevered colour now high in her cheeks as she turned away. 'Accompany me back to Lady Stockton's ballroom, if you please, Lord Anthony,' she requested stiffly as she left Darian's side to walk quickly down the gallery to take the arm his brother so gallantly offered her.

Anthony paused to give Darian a warning glance over the top of Mariah's averted head. 'I have changed my mind, Darian, and we will now talk again later tonight, rather than tomorrow morning.'

Darian recognised those words for exactly what they were: a threat, not a promise.

Chapter Four

Darian found himself seated beside the fire at
his club the following afternoon, after partak-
ing of luncheon with two of his closest friends;
Christian Seaton, the Duke of Sutherland, and
Griffin Stone, the Duke of Rotherham.

'You are saying the countess refused to see you
when you called at Carlisle House this morning?'
Sutherland prompted lightly.

Darian scowled into the depths of his brandy
glass. 'Her butler claimed she was indisposed
and not receiving visitors.'

'Women do tend to suffer these indelicacies,
you know.' Rotherham nodded dismissively.

The scowl remained on Darian's brow as he
looked across the fireplace at his friend slumped
in the chair opposite. 'So you think the indispo-

sition might be genuine, rather than an excuse not to see me in particular?'

'Well, I would not go quite so far as to say that,' Rotherham drawled. 'From what you told us over luncheon, you did make rather a cake of yourself, you know, throwing out accusations and insults in that overbearing manner of yours!'

Darian gave a wince. 'Thank you so much for your reassurances, Griff.' After Anthony's promised late visit to Wolfingham House the night before, Darian had every reason to know he had indeed made a cake of himself where Mariah Beecham was concerned and certainly did not need Rotherham to tell him as much.

The need to apologise to Mariah was the very reason Darian had attempted to call upon her this morning. Only to be sent away by her butler without so much as a glimpse of the lady, let alone be allowed to give the apology owed to her.

'Think nothing of it, old boy.' Rotherham grinned across at him unabashedly.

'Beautiful woman, the countess,' Sutherland murmured appreciatively as he relaxed in a third chair.

'Oh, yes!' Rotherham nodded.

Darian eyed the two men sharply. 'Have either of you…?' He could not quite bring himself to say the words; the thought that Sutherland or Rotherham might have been Mariah's lover was enough to blacken his mood even more than it already was.

'Never had the pleasure.' Sutherland sighed his obvious disappointment.

'Unfortunately not.' Rotherham looked equally as wistful.

Darian found himself breathing a little easier at knowing that two of his friends, at least, had never been one of Mariah Beecham's lovers. Even if rumour suggested that plenty of other gentlemen had!

'I suppose there is always the possibility the countess was not actually *at* home when you called this morning?' Sutherland quirked a brow. 'You did say she was rather pally with Maystone yesterday evening, so perhaps she went home with him? Just a thought.' He shrugged dismissively as Darian's scowl deepened.

'The idea did occur to me.' Of course it had occurred to him that Mariah might have spent the night elsewhere than her London home.

Until he had remembered that Mariah had accompanied her young daughter to the Stockton ball and so was hardly likely to have abandoned that young lady in favour of going home with a lover.

Of course Mariah could have gone out again once she had returned Lady Christina to Carlisle House.

He shifted restlessly, aware that he was taking far too much of an interest in front of his two friends, who along with himself were the last of the bachelor Dangerous Dukes, in what Mariah Beecham did or did not do.

'Do you have hopes in that direction yourself?' Sutherland now arched a curious brow.

Did he?

Darian had been unable to sleep last night for thinking of Mariah, of holding her in his arms and kissing her.

Of his desire for her!

A desire he had neither sought nor wanted.

Because every objection he had given Anthony

for his brother to bring an end to his involvement with Mariah Beecham—apart from the difference in their ages—also applied to Darian himself. An association, any association on his part with the notorious Mariah Beecham, was unacceptable.

A realisation that seemed not to make a bit of difference to the desire Darian felt for her and that had so disturbed his sleep the night before.

Oh, it was perfectly acceptable for Darian to take a mistress if he so chose, even if he had never chosen to do so before now. But Mariah Beecham, a woman whose private life was gossiped and speculated about constantly, was not suitable even for that role in the public *or* private life of the Duke of Wolfingham.

His continuing work for the Crown had caused Darian to long ago make a conscious decision not to bring any unnecessary attention to his private life. And any liaison with Mariah Beecham would necessarily become public and ultimately throw him front and centre of the same gossip that always surrounded her. Gossip Darian wished to avoid, even if Mariah had been willing to enter into such a relationship with him.

Which Darian had every reason to believe, to *know*—more so than ever, after his clarifying conversation with Anthony the night before—she was not!

So Darian had told himself again and again, as he lay in his bed unable to sleep the previous night.

Today, with the disappointment of not being able to see and speak with Mariah this morning, as he had fully intended that he would, he was not so sure on the matter.

'Of course not,' he answered Sutherland sharply. 'I am merely aware that I owe the woman an apology and I am anxious to get it over and done with.'

'Protesting a little too strongly, do you think, Sutherland?' Griffin Stone turned to prompt the other man drily.

'More than a little, I would say,' Sutherland drawled as they both turned to look at Darian, brows raised over mocking eyes.

Darian withstood that look with a censorious

one of his own, having every intention of making his apologies to Mariah Beecham before returning to their previous relationship—that of complete indifference to each other.

Something Darian very much doubted was going to happen, on his part at least, when he was shown into the gold salon of Mariah's home late the following morning and his rebellious body responded immediately.

He had wisely sent her a note late yesterday afternoon, requesting she supply a suitable time for him to call upon her today, rather than run the risk of calling and being turned away for a second time.

Mariah looked ethereally beautiful this morning, in a fashionable gown of the palest lemon, her blonde curls a golden halo about the pale delicacy of her face and throat.

A pallor that implied that perhaps Mariah's claim, of being indisposed yesterday, had indeed been genuine?

'Are you feeling any better today?' Darian prompted gruffly as he crossed the room to where she now stood, taking the gloved hand she raised to him in formal greeting.

'Such politeness, Wolfingham. Indeed, I should hardly recognise you,' Mariah taunted drily as she deftly removed her hand from his before resuming her seat, the gold brocade sofa a perfect foil for her golden loveliness. Deliberately so?

His mouth thinned. 'Could we perhaps at least attempt a modicum of politeness between the two of us, rather than begin to argue immediately after we see each other again?'

'I do not believe it is a question of us arguing, Wolfingham. We simply do not like each other!'

He drew in a sharp breath, knowing that for his part that claim was untrue, that he liked—indeed, he *desired*—Mariah Beecham far more than was comfortable.

Mariah studied Wolfingham from beneath lowered lashes as he made no reply to her taunt.

It had been her dearest wish never to find herself alone with this gentleman again. She had only agreed to this morning's meeting because she knew he was not a man she could continue to avoid indefinitely, if he had decided it should

be otherwise. Her claim of being indisposed yesterday, as a way of avoiding Wolfingham when
he called, had not been all fabrication; Mariah
had stayed in her bed late yesterday morning,
her head aching after suffering a restless and
sleepless night.

Because she had not been able to stop thinking of Darian Hunter. Or his having kissed her.

Or remembering that she had responded.

A response that was so unprecedented, and had
troubled Mariah so deeply, that she had found
it impossible to sleep these past two nights for
thinking of it.

A response she had since assured herself would
not happen again.

Could not happen again!

So it was entirely frustrating for her to ac-
knowledge her awareness of how arrogantly
handsome Wolfingham looked this morning,
dressed in a dark green superfine and buff-and-
green-striped waistcoat, his linen snowy white,
buff-coloured pantaloons moulded to the muscular length of his long thighs above his brown-
topped black Hessians. His hair was in its usual

fashionable disarray about his sharply etched features.

As she also noted the pallor to those sharply etched features and the dark shadows beneath his deep green eyes. As evidence, perhaps, that Wolfingham had not rested any better than she had herself these past two nights?

Although she doubted it was for the same reasons.

Against all the odds—her dislike of Wolfingham and the years of her unhappy marriage to Martin—for the first time in her life Mariah had found herself actually enjoying being held in a man's arms two nights ago.

Even more surprising was the realisation of how she had *responded* to that depth of passion Wolfingham had ignited in her.

Her marriage to Martin had been completely without love and affection from the onset, on either side, and equally as without passion. Indeed, for the first ten years of their marriage, the two of them had spent very little time even living in the same house, Mariah languishing in the country with their daughter, while Martin preferred to spend most of the year living in London. At best they had been polite strangers to each other on the rare occasions they did meet, for the sake of their daughter, and more often than not they had ignored each other completely.

That had changed slightly seven years ago, when Mariah began to spend the Season in London, Martin necessarily having to accompany her to at least some of those social engagements. But even so, those occasions had only been for appearances' sake, and they had continued to retain their separate bedchambers, and for the most part live their separate lives, on the occasions they were forced to reside in the same house together.

So, it had been all the more surprising to Mariah that she had not only responded to, but enjoyed being held in Darian Hunter's arms and being kissed by him, the night of Lady Stockton's ball. Not only an unprecedented response, but an unwanted one as well, and ensuring that Mariah was all the more determined it would not occur for a second time.

'Did you have something in particular you

wished to discuss with me when you called upon me yesterday morning, then sent a note requesting a convenient time you might call again today? Or is it as I suspected and you merely wish to add to the insults you invariably make when we meet?'

Darian's breath left him in a hiss at this deliberate challenge; at least when he was breathing out his senses were not being invaded by Mariah Beecham's heady and arousing perfume.

Darian had once again been aware of that perfume the moment he stepped into the salon. Indeed, he believed he now knew that unique aroma so well he would be able to pick Mariah Beecham out of a roomful of veiled and heavily robed women, just by the smell of that heady perfume alone.

Seeing Mariah again this morning, being with her again, his senses once again invaded by her beauty and aroused by that heady perfume, made a complete nonsense of his denials of yesterday to Rotherham and Sutherland, in regard to his not having the slightest interest in pursuing a relationship with Mariah Beecham.

He might not *want* to feel this desire for her, but he did feel it nonetheless.

'Oh, do stop scowling, Wolfingham, for it is giving me a headache,' Mariah snapped at his continued silence. 'I am sure there are many women who might find all this brooding intensity attractive, but I am not one of them.' She wrinkled her nose in disgust. 'Personally, such behaviour has always filled me with a burning desire to administer a weighty smack to the cheek of the gentleman in question.'

The situation in which Darian currently found himself did not at all call for any sign of levity on his part. Consequently he did try very hard not to give in to the laughter that threatened to burst forth.

To no avail, unfortunately; his amusement was such that it refused to be denied and he found himself chuckling with husky appreciation for Mariah's obviously heartfelt sentiments.

'You are incorrigible, madam,' he admonished once he had regained his breath enough to speak.

'I, sir, merely remain unimpressed by any gentleman's angst,' Mariah returned disparagingly.

'But more so when that gentleman is me,' Wolfingham acknowledged drily.

'Yes.' She did not even attempt to deny it as she gave an impatient shake of her head. 'It was *you* who asked if you might call upon me today, Wolfingham, so I ask once again that you state your business and then leave. I find maintaining even this level of politeness between the two of us to be taxing in the extreme.'

Darian knew he fully deserved Mariah's lack of enjoyment of his company. He had made so many mistakes in their short acquaintance, it seemed. Too many for her to forgive him? Easily, if at all.

He drew in a deep breath. 'I needed to speak with you again because it appears that I owe you an apology, Mariah.'

Her eyes widened in obvious surprise. 'Indeed?'

His jaw grated he held it so tightly clenched. 'Yes.'

'For what, pray? You have made far too many insults, to me and about me, for me to ever be able to pick out a specific one for which you might apologise.'

Darian bristled. 'Such as?'

'The disgusting thoughts you so obviously held two evenings ago, with regard to my friendship with Aubrey Maystone, for one.'

Ah. Yes. Well, there was that, of course...

He shifted uncomfortably. 'It was a natural conclusion to have come to, surely, given the circumstances of the ease of the friendship between the two of you?'

'Only if your mind was already in the gutter, as yours so often appears to be where I am concerned!' Her eyes flashed.

Darian could not deny that he had thought the worst of Mariah before he had even met her, hence his initial alarm regarding Anthony's involvement with her. But in his defence Mariah Beecham's reputation in society was such that surely, at the time, he could have formed no other opinion, in regard to Anthony's obvious and public attentions to her.

At the time.

Darian knew differently now, of course. Which

was the very reason he had been so determined to speak with Mariah these past two days. So that he might apologise and, hopefully, discuss the matter with her further.

'It was doubly insulting, when you had already accused me of being involved in an affair with your younger brother,' she now accused coldly.

And now, Darian recognised heavily, was the perfect opportunity in which to make that apology and inform her of his mistake.

He grimaced. 'I have had the opportunity to speak with Anthony again, since the two of us parted so badly at the Stockton ball.' He ignored her scathing snort; she knew as well as he did that it had been Anthony's parting remark— promise—that had caused the two brothers to talk again later that very same night. 'And it would seem—it would seem—'

Darian was not accustomed to apologising for his actions, to anyone, and yet in this particular instance he knew he had no choice; he had seriously wronged Mariah and now he must apologise for it.

He sighed. 'My brother has now made it more

than clear to me that his affections lie elsewhere than yourself.'

'Hah!' Those turquoise-blue eyes gleamed across at him with triumphant satisfaction. 'Did I not tell you that you were mistaken in your accusations?'

'It is very unbecoming in a woman to say "I told you so" in that gleeful manner, Mariah.' Darian scowled, still more than a little irritated with himself for having initially jumped to the wrong conclusion where his brother's affections were concerned, and even more so for having then acted upon those conclusions by insulting Mariah to such a degree he now owed her an apology.

He was equally as irritated that by doing so he had now placed himself in the position of being the one to tell Mariah the truth of that situation.

'Not when that woman has been proved right and you have been proved wrong.' she came back tartly.

Darian chose his words carefully. 'I was only half-wrong—'

'How can a person, even the illustrious and arrogant Duke of Wolfingham, be half-wrong?' she scorned. 'Admit it, Wolfingham. In this matter you were completely and utterly in the wrong.'

'No, I was not.' Darian sighed deeply, choosing to ignore the scathing comment in regard to himself; no doubt Mariah would have more, far stronger insults to hurl at him before this conversation was over. 'I was merely mistaken as to which of the Beecham ladies held Anthony's affections and consequently, the reason for his polite and public attentions to you.'

He also had absolutely no idea how Mariah was going to react upon learning that Anthony was paying court to her young daughter, Christina, rather than to herself. Even if he only took into consideration Mariah's feelings towards *him*, Anthony's despicable and insulting older brother, then Darian was sure that it could not be in a favourable way.

Any more than were his own feelings on the matter. Admittedly, he could not help but feel a certain amount of relief at having learnt that Anthony was not besotted with Mariah Beecham, after all. For the reasons he had previously stated.

But also on a personal level.

Unwanted as his own desire for Mariah might be, Darian nevertheless felt a certain relief at knowing he was not harbouring a desire for the same woman for whom he had believed his brother had serious intentions.

As for the real object of his brother's affections…

Admittedly the seventeen-year-old Lady Christina Beecham was more acceptable as a wife for Anthony than her mother could ever have been. But, in Darian's opinion, only marginally so. Christina Beecham could not escape the fact that she was the daughter of a woman with a notorious and scandalous reputation.

A woman with a notorious and scandalous reputation who, he realised belatedly, for the moment seemed to have been struck uncharacteristically dumb. At having learnt that his brother, Anthony's, romantic inclinations were directed towards her young daughter rather than herself?

Mariah drew a harsh breath into her starved lungs as she realised she had forgotten to do so these past few seconds. 'Forgive me, but I— Am

I to understand that your brother, Lord Anthony Hunter, a gentleman aged almost five and twenty, believes himself to be in love with—that he has serious intentions towards my seventeen-year-old daughter?'

Wolfingham gave a terse nod of his head. 'That is exactly what I am saying, yes. I have no reason to believe that your daughter returns Anthony's feelings.' His eyes narrowed. 'But perhaps you do?'

'Not as such, no.'

'You seem unduly concerned?'

'She is seventeen years of age, Wolfingham. At the very least Christina will have been flattered by the attentions of an eligible and sophisticated gentleman such as your brother,' Mariah answered distractedly as she now recalled all those occasions these past few weeks when Lord Anthony Hunter had been included in the group of admirers surrounding herself and Christina.

As she also remembered the polite attentions the young Lord Anthony had paid to her and the visits he had made to Carlisle House—and that Wolfingham had mistaken for a romantic interest in Mariah—in an effort, no doubt, to ingratiate himself into Mariah's good opinion.

And Christina's youthful heart?

The more Mariah considered the matter, the more she believed that her daughter could not help but be aware of Anthony Hunter's romantic interest in her.

Having spent much of Christina's early years closeted alone together in the country, Mariah believed she and Christina were closer than most mothers and daughters of the *ton*. But Christina was fully grown now—or believed that she was!—and Mariah now realised that those childhood confidences had become fewer and fewer during these past few weeks spent together in London.

Perhaps because Christina harboured a secret passion for her handsome admirer?

A secret passion that, because of her age, she knew Mariah could not, and would not, approve of?

Oh, she had been unable to deny Christina her first Season; her daughter was seventeen, after all. But Mariah had not launched Christina into society with any intentions of seeing her young daughter engaged to be married within weeks of her having made that appearance.

As she herself had been.

Mariah gave a determined shake of her head. 'Whether she does or does not, it will not do, Wolfingham.'

He arched dark brows. 'You would refuse Anthony's suit?'

'Her uncle, the earl, is her male guardian, but I will strongly advise against it, yes.'

'Why would you?' Having been so set against the match himself, Darian now felt contrarily defensive on his brother's behalf. Anthony might be young, and occasionally irresponsible, but none could doubt his eligibility in the marriage mart. 'Lady Christina is seventeen years of age—'

'And so far too young to fall in love, or consider taking on the duties of marriage!' Mariah scorned.

'Surely she is the same age as you must have been when you married?'

'We were not discussing me!' Those turquoise-coloured eyes now glittered fiercely across the room at him.

Wolfingham's gaze became quizzical at her vehemence. 'I thought an advantageous marriage was the whole purpose of a young lady making her debut in society?'

'That is a typically male assessment of the situation.'

He arched a dark brow. 'Then perhaps it is that you consider that having a daughter married to be ageing to yourself?'

'Do not be any more ridiculous than you have already been, Wolfingham!' Mariah stood up agitatedly. 'My reservations have absolutely nothing to do with myself and everything to do with Christina. She is far too young to know her own mind in such matters.'

'She seemed a prepossessing young lady when I danced with her the other evening.'

'So she is.' Mariah nodded her impatience. 'And no doubt I will one day, in the distant future, be happy to dance at her wedding. But not now, when Christina has only been out for a matter of weeks, rather than years. Nor do I have any reason to believe that you would approve of an alliance between your brother and my daughter?' She looked up at him challengingly.

No, of course Darian did not approve of it and he had voiced his reservations regarding the match to his brother when the two of them had spoken so frankly together two evenings ago. A disapproval that Darian knew had once again fallen on deaf ears; Anthony was bound and determined in his pursuit of Christina Beecham.

A determination that was obviously to now be thwarted by that young lady's mother.

Again, Darian found himself playing devil's advocate. 'I still fail to see, apart from your daughter's youth, what your own objections can be to the match. Anthony will come into his own fortune on the occasion of his twenty-fifth birthday in just a few months' time. He is the grandson, the son and now the brother of a duke—'

'I am fully aware of who Lord Anthony is and of his family connections,' Mariah assured him dismissively.

'And the fact that the severe and sober Duke of Wolfingham is his brother is no doubt part of

the reason for your own objections to the match?'
Darian surmised drily.

'Do not even pretend to be insulted, Wolfingham, when you know full well your feelings
on this matter entirely match my own.' Mariah
sighed her impatience.

'I repeat, why are they?'

Mariah drew in a deep and controlling breath,
knowing she was overreacting to this situation,
allowing her own unhappy marriage at the age
of seventeen, the same age as her daughter was
now, to colour her judgement. And in front of the
astute and intelligent Darian Hunter, of all people. 'Of course I wish for Christina's future happiness. Just not yet. She is so young and has not
yet had chance to enjoy even her first Season.'

'Is it only because he is my younger brother?'
he guessed shrewdly.

Mariah gave a determined shake of her head. 'I
also have no doubt that, if Christina were ever to
become your brother's wife, you would make her
life, as your sister-in-law, nothing but a misery.'

He stiffened. 'You are insulting, madam, to believe I would ever treat any woman so shabbily.'

'You would treat any daughter of *mine* more than shabbily,' she insisted. 'And I do not want that for Christina. She deserves so much more than that.' So much more than Mariah had suffered herself as Martin's wife, unloved by her husband and disapproved of and ignored by his family for her more humble beginnings. 'No.' She shuddered at the thought of Christina suffering the same fate. 'If Lord Anthony should ask, I will not ever give my blessing to such a match.'

Darian frowned darkly. 'And what of your daughter's feelings on the matter? Have you considered that perhaps she might return Anthony's affections? If not now, then at some future date?'

'It is perhaps a possibility that she may one day *believe* she returns those feelings,' Mariah allowed grudgingly. 'But at seventeen she is too young to know her own heart and mind.'

'As you yourself were at the same age?'

She stiffened. 'Again, we were not talking about me.'

'Then perhaps we should be.'

'No, we will not,' Mariah informed Wolfingham coldly. 'Not now, nor at any time in the future.'

Darian studied Mariah intently, knowing by the stubborn set of her mouth, and those flashing turquoise eyes, that she would not be moved on the subject of her own marriage.

And so adding to the mystery that Mariah Beecham had become to him.

A mystery that had already occupied far too much of his time and thoughts these past ten days.

He gave a grimace. 'Have you considered how your husband might have felt regarding an alliance between his daughter and the Hunter family?'

Her chin rose. 'I had no interest in my husband's opinions whilst he was alive and I certainly have none now that he is dead.'

Because, as he had begun to suspect, like so many marriages of the *ton*, the Beecham marriage had been one of convenience rather than a love match? A question of marrying wealth to a title? The wealth of Mariah's father matched to Beecham's title as the Earl of Carlisle?

Darian's own parents had married under similar circumstances, but they had been two of the lucky ones, in that they had come to feel a deep love and respect for each other, ensuring that their two sons had grown up in a family filled with that same love and respect.

The fact that Mariah had only been seventeen to Beecham's two and forty when their marriage took place, and the rumours of her numerous affairs since, would seem to imply she might not have been so fortunate.

'That is a very enlightening comment,' he said slowly.

'Is it?' Mariah returned scathingly. 'I doubt I am the first woman to admit to having felt a lack of love for the man who was her husband.'

'Your words implied a lack of respect, too.'

Those eyes flashed again. 'Respect has to be earned. It is not just given.'

'And Carlisle did not earn yours?'

'The feeling was mutual, I assure you.'

'And yet the two of you had a daughter together.'

A cold shiver ran down the length of Mariah's

spine as she remembered the night of Christina's conception. A painful and frightening experience for Mariah and a triumphant one for Martin.

Her gaze now avoided Wolfingham's probing green one. 'I believe it is time you left.'

'Mariah—'

'*Now*, Wolfingham!' Before Mariah broke down completely. Something she dared not do, in front of the one man who had already somehow managed to get through the barrier Mariah had long ago placed about both her emotions and the memories of the past. For fear they might destroy her utterly.

Darian had no idea what would have happened next. Whether he would have acceded to Mariah's request for him to leave, or whether he would have followed his own instincts and instead taken Mariah in his arms and comforted her. This talk of her marriage to Carlisle seemed to have shaken her cool self-confidence in a way nothing else had.

Instead, their privacy was interrupted as the butler entered the room bearing a card upon a silver tray, which he proceeded to present to Mariah.

She picked up the card and quickly read it, before tucking it into the pocket of her gown as she spoke to her butler. 'Please show his Lordship into my private parlour, Fuller,' she instructed briskly. 'And then return here and show his Grace out.' Her gaze was challenging as she turned and waited for the butler to leave before looking across the room at Darian.

Darian breathed out his frustration, both with what was obviously Mariah's dismissal of him and a burning curiosity to know the identity of the man the dismissed butler was even now escorting to Mariah's private parlour.

Which was utterly ridiculous of him.

He had lived for two and thirty years without having the slightest interest in Mariah Beecham, or any of her friendships, and for him to now feel disgruntled, even jealous, of this other man was ludicrous on his part.

And yet Darian could not deny that was exactly how he now felt.

Just as he knew Mariah was equally as determined that her two male visitors would not meet each other.

'I believe I am perfectly capable of showing myself out, Mariah,' Darian informed her harshly.

She blinked. 'Fuller will return in just a moment.'

'And I am ready to depart now.'

'But—'

'Good day to you, Mariah.' Darian bowed to her stiffly before crossing the room and stepping out into the cavernous hallway, only to come to an abrupt halt as he saw the identity of Mariah's caller.

'Wolfingham!' Lord Aubrey Maystone turned at the bottom of the staircase to greet him enthusiastically; eyes alight with pleasure as he strode forward to shake Darian warmly by the hand. 'How fortuitous this is, for you are just the man I wanted to see.'

Darian failed to see how that was possible, when Maystone could not have had any idea that Darian would be at Mariah Beecham's home this morning.

Or could he?

As Darian knew only too well, from working so closely with the older man for so many years, Maystone was deceptively wily. A man capable of weaving webs within webs and all without losing sight of a single thread of those intricate weavings.

Although Darian seriously doubted that the other man's role as spymaster was his reason for calling upon Mariah this morning.

Indeed, Mariah's instruction, for Maystone to be taken to her private parlour, left only one conclusion in regard to Maystone's presence here this morning: that the older man was indeed the man Mariah was currently intimately involved with and his joviality was now merely a politeness in front of Mariah's butler.

Chapter Five

Mariah had hurriedly followed Wolfingham out into the entrance hall and had arrived just in time to witness Aubrey Maystone warmly greeting and shaking the younger man by the hand. Much, she noted ruefully, to Darian Hunter's stony-faced displeasure.

No doubt because Wolfingham had now deduced, despite her denials to the contrary, that she was indeed involved in an affair with Aubrey Maystone.

Just as she was sure that Aubrey Mayston's real reason for calling upon her so unexpectedly this morning was sure to be a matter of some delicacy and no doubt related to her work for the Crown.

In which case, the arrogantly disapproving

Darian Hunter would just have to continue to think what he would regarding her relationship with the older man. As, it seemed, he always chose to think the worst of her.

'Aubrey!' She greeted the older man with a warm smile as she crossed the hallway to link her arm with his and allowed him to kiss her lightly on the cheek. 'His Grace was just leaving.' She turned to look at Wolfingham with coldly challenging eyes.

'I would prefer him to remain, my dear.'

To Mariah's surprise it was Aubrey Maystone who answered her softly, rather than the harsh response she had fully expected from Wolfingham regarding her obvious dismissal of him. A frown marred her brow as she turned to give the older man a puzzled glance.

Maystone raised his brows pointedly towards her hovering butler before answering her. 'Might I suggest you consider ordering us all some refreshment?'

'Er—of course.' Mariah was more than a little disconcerted. 'Bring tea and brandy, if you please, Fuller,' she instructed distractedly before the three of them turned to enter the gold salon. Mariah was still totally at a loss to understand why Aubrey Maystone should have deliberately delayed Wolfingham's departure.

'What is this all about, Maystone?' Darian Hunter felt no hesitation in expressing his own impatience with the older man's request, as he restlessly paced the length of the room once the three of them were alone together with the door closed behind them. A disdainful smile curled his top lip. 'I trust we are not about to engage in a proprietary claim of ownership on your part, in response to your having discovered my having paid the countess a visit this morning?'

'Wolfingham!' the older man snapped reprovingly.

Mariah also gasped at Wolfingham's deliberate insult. 'I am not a hunting dog, nor a piece of horseflesh, Wolfingham, to be *owned* by any man!'

In truth, it had not been Darian's intention to insult Mariah. He had merely meant to challenge the older man for what he perceived must be

Maystone's displeasure at finding Darian in the home of his mistress.

Darian had not *meant* to insult Mariah, but he could see by the stiff way that she now held herself, the fierce glitter in her eyes and the two spots of angry colour that had appeared in her otherwise pale cheeks, that was exactly what he had done. 'I meant you no disrespect—'

'Did you not?' she scorned.

Had he?

Darian frowned as he realised that *he* was the one who felt displeased and unsettled, both at the other man's arrival and the unmistakable familiarity that he knew existed between Maystone and Mariah.

It was obvious, from the warmth of Mariah's tone and manner whenever she spoke to the older man, that she liked and approved of Aubrey Maystone. Just as it was equally as obvious, from the coldness of her tone and manner whenever she addressed Darian, that she disliked and disapproved of *him* intensely.

And he, Darian acknowledged heavily, had done little in their acquaintance so far to dispel or temper those feelings of dislike. The opposite, in fact. 'I sincerely apologise if I spoke out of turn.' He bowed stiffly to Mariah before turning to the older man. 'Perhaps, if you have something you wish to say to me, Maystone, it might be better if we arrange another time and place in which to have that conversation?'

'I trust you are not considering engaging in *another* duel, Wolfingham?' Mariah Beecham scorned.

'Another duel?' Lord Maystone looked confused.

'A misunderstanding on Lady Beecham's part,' Darian dismissed coolly; Aubrey Maystone was one of the few people who knew in exactly what manner Darian had received the bullet wound to his shoulder. 'If you will send word when it is convenient for me to call upon you, Maystone?'

'I was perfectly serious when I said it was fortuitous that you happened to be here this morning.' The older man eyed him impatiently.

Darian studied the older man through narrowed lids, noting the hard glitter to Maystone's eyes and the lines of strain etched beside his nose and mouth. Evidence that the other man's mood was not as cheerfully relaxed as it had appeared to be when he had arrived? 'What could you possibly have to discuss with me if not my visit this morning to Mar—Lady Beecham?'

Mariah was wondering the same thing, as she also wondered why Aubrey Maystone had called at her home at all; as a precaution, the two of them had never met at Aubrey's offices in the Foreign Office or here in her home, but chose instead to pass information on to each other whenever Aubrey arranged for them to meet socially. The fact that Aubrey had chosen to call on her here this morning must mean that he had something of a serious nature to import.

Although that still did not explain why it was he wished Wolfingham to remain.

'That will be all, thank you, Fuller.' Mariah smiled at the butler once he had straightened from placing the tray bearing the tea and brandy on the low coffee table. 'I am not at home to any more callers this morning,' she added, waiting until her butler had left the room and closed the door behind him before turning back to Aubrey Maystone. 'What—'

'I shall begin this conversation,' Maystone spoke firmly, 'by first stating that it is necessary that I now inform both of you of the other's involvement in certain matters of secrecy and delicacy to the Crown.'

Mariah was so stunned by Aubrey's announcement that she instantly sank down weakly into one of the armchairs, before she even dared to look up and see that Wolfingham's expression was one of equal shock—proof that he was just as stunned as she was at being so bluntly outed as an agent for the Crown, by the very man who acted as her—no, their?—spymaster?

Mariah was more than shocked; she was having great difficulty believing Aubrey Maystone's announcement in regard to the haughtily disapproving and condescending Duke of Wolfingham.

The man Mariah knew society believed to be both sober and stern.

A man she personally knew to be arrogant and unpleasant, as well as insulting.

That same gentleman worked secretly, as she did, for the Crown?

It seemed barely possible it could be true, yet it must be so if Aubrey Maystone said that it was.

The puzzle was why Aubrey Maystone had now revealed something that had, in Mariah's case, remained a secret to all but her daughter for seven years.

A sentiment, a confidence, that Wolfingham echoed, if the glittering green of his eyes was any indication. 'What do you mean by talking so frankly, Maystone?'

'Recent developments have made it necessary, Darian,' the older man excused heavily as he gave a dismissive wave of his hand. 'And I also suggest that the two of you get over your shock as quickly as possible, so that we might then proceed.'

Darian *was* shocked by Maystone's unexpected announcement, too much so to be able to hide the emotion.

And it was a knowledge, in regard to Mariah Beecham, that instantly posed a dozen other questions in Darian's mind.

Such as how long had Mariah been engaged in such dangerous and secret work for the Crown?

And why had she?

When did she?

Where?

And how?

It was perhaps the answer to that last question that interested Darian the most.

For surely there was only one way in which a woman in society might go about gaining secret information?

'It would seem, Aubrey, that Wolfingham is too busy drawing his own conclusions as to the methods I might utilise—flirtation, teasing, *seduction*—in order to be able to garner that information, to be able to proceed at the moment,' Mariah drawled coldly, for once Wolfingham's thoughts having been crystal clear to her. Unpleasantly so!

He scowled. 'I was merely—'

'I am well aware of what you were *merely thinking*, Wolfingham,' she snapped disgustedly.

His jaw tightened. 'Do not presume to know the thoughts in my head, madam—'

'Enough,' the older man interrupted wearily. 'We do not have time for petty arguments this morning.'

Those green eyes turned as hard as the emeralds they resembled as Wolfingham turned his attention back to the other man. 'Then perhaps you might state what it is we do need to talk about so urgently that you have deliberately chosen to put both myself and Lady Beecham in a position of personal vulnerability?'

'Only to each other.'

'Exactly!' Wolfingham scowled darkly.

Maystone grimaced. 'It was necessary, Darian.'

'As I said, I would be interested to know why.'

'Plots and treason, Wolfingham,' Maystone stated emphatically.

'There is always talk of plots and treason,' Wolfingham dismissed scathingly.

'This time it is different.' The older man frowned darkly. 'Perhaps you will better understand the situation if I tell you that in the past week plots to assassinate the tsar and the Austrian emperor have been discovered and the assassins dealt with. That such a plot, despite all our efforts to make it otherwise, still exists in regard to our own Prince Regent.'

'Good lord!' Wolfingham slowly lowered his body down into one of the armchairs, his face pale.

Maystone nodded. 'Five days ago two people, a tutor and a footman, attached to and working in the households of two prominent politicians, were taken in for questioning on the matter. My own private secretary was taken into custody late last night,' Maystone continued grimly. 'And he is even now being questioned as to the part he has played in the plot to assassinate the Regent himself.'

'How is such a thing possible?' Mariah breathed faintly, her hand shaking as she lifted it to her mouth.

Maystone gave Darian a telling glance. 'I am sure *you*, at least, will better understand the seriousness of this threat if I say that your old friend Rousseau was involved?'

Both men were well aware that the Frenchman was no friend of Darian's. Indeed, Rousseau was responsible for the bullet wound in Darian's shoulder. As Darian was responsible for having brought the other man's life to a swift and sudden end.

He gave a shake of his head. 'He left England and returned to France almost a year ago.'

'But not before he had set up a network of his own spies and assassins amongst the households of some of the leading members of the English government,' Maystone rasped disgustedly. 'All set in place and ready to act when or if Napoleon departed Elba and attempted to return to France as emperor, which, as we all know, he is currently doing. At which time the heads of the allied countries were to be eliminated, an act designed to throw the governments of the alliance into chaos.'

Darian lay his head back against the chair and closed his eyes, better understanding the reason for Maystone's agitation now. Such a plot as the other man was outlining could have had, might still have, a devastating effect on the shaky alliance formed against Napoleon.

Especially so, as Napoleon was even now

marching triumphantly towards Paris, an army of hundreds of thousands at his back. And all without, as Napoleon had claimed it would be, a shot being fired.

'How was it even possible for a Frenchman to do such a thing?' Mariah frowned.

Maystone gave a humourless grimace. 'Because he worked and lived in England for a year under the guise of tutor to a son of a member of the aristocracy. Jeffrey Lancaster, the future heir and now the Earl of Malvern, to be exact.'

'You are referring to the French tutor the Lancaster chit eloped with last year?' Mariah gasped. 'Does it surprise you, knowing what you do now, that I have made a point of knowing these things?' she added dismissively as Wolfingham gave her a frowning glance.

'That "Lancaster chit" is now the Duchess of Hawksmere and the wife of a close friend of mine!' he reminded stiffly.

'She was also the lover of this man, André Rousseau, for several months, if I am to understand this situation correctly,' Mariah maintained stubbornly.

'Situations are not always as they appear.'

'As I once reminded you,' Mariah said pointedly 'You—'

'Could we please concentrate on the subject at hand?' Maystone interrupted irritably, before sighing heavily. 'Yes, my dear Mariah, for the sake of clarity, I can confirm that you are quite correct in believing that André Rousseau was tutor to young Jeffrey Lancaster for a year and also the same man who persuaded Lancaster's sister Georgianna into eloping with him. I would like to add in her defence,' he continued firmly, 'that she was also responsible for bringing us information vital to our government just weeks ago. Information that also resulted in Rousseau's death in Paris just fifteen days ago.'

'Fifteen days ago?' Mariah did a quick calculation in her head as she recalled that it had been nine days ago that Wolfingham had told her he had been shot 'six days ago, to be precise'.

It did not take a genius to add nine and six together and come up with the correct answer.

She slowly turned to look at Wolfingham, knowing by the challenging glitter in those emerald-green eyes as he returned her gaze, that her calculations were correct.

Wolfingham had killed André Rousseau in Paris fifteen days ago.

And in doing so he had received a bullet wound to his shoulder.

She had no doubt now that Darian Hunter, the haughty Duke of Wolfingham, was not only a spy for the Crown, as she was, but that he had also travelled to France in the past three weeks, in the midst of the turmoil of the Corsican's escape and return to France, and succeeded in killing the man who was a known spy for Napoleon.

As Wolfingham had killed others, in the past, who had threatened the security of the Crown?

It was both shocking and a little daunting to realise there was so much more to the Duke of Wolfingham than the disdain he chose to show outwardly and those flashes of passion he had so ably demonstrated to Mariah privately.

So much so that Mariah now viewed him with new and wary eyes. She had already considered her unwanted physical response to Darian Hunter to be a risk to her peace of mind, but this new information, on exactly what sort of a man the Duke of Wolfingham really was, now caused Mariah to consider him as being completely dangerous.

Indeed, he reminded her of a stalking predator, a wolf, hiding behind a mask of stern urbanity.

Proof indeed that he had more than earned his place as being thought of as one of the five Dangerous Dukes.

'If we could return to the more immediate problem of this plot to assassinate the Regent?' Lord Maystone prompted drily as he obviously saw this silent battle of wills between Mariah and Wolfingham.

Mariah found it hard to breathe, let alone break away from that glittering green gaze, feeling as if she were a butterfly stuck on the end of a pin and with no way of escape.

She began to breathe again only when Darian Hunter, after giving her a hard and mocking smile, turned his attention back to Aubrey Maystone.

'I am presuming that your own private secretary's involvement with Rousseau will also have exposed the names of the network of people who work for you?' Wolfingham prompted astutely.

Mariah's eyes widened in alarm as she saw the truth of that statement in the heavy mantle of responsibility that instantly settled on Aubrey Maystone's slumped and aged shoulders.

'Almost all.' The older man nodded. 'We had our first inkling of that exposure, of course, when Rousseau revealed to Georgianna Lancaster that he knew of Hawksmere's work for the Crown.'

Darian nodded grimly, that information having meant that Hawksmere could no longer play an active role in Maystone's network of spies. Perhaps it was as well, now that Hawksmere was a married man, but even so...

'I am also presuming, as you wished to speak with both of us this morning, that perhaps Lady Beecham and myself have so far not been exposed?'

'That is so, yes,' Maystone confirmed tightly. 'I do not keep written records of my agents, as you know, but of the twelve in my network, only the two of you have never had reason to call at the Foreign Office or my home.'

'And would not the fact that you have chosen to call at the countess's home this morning have succeeded in alerting any now watching you to the possibility that she—'

'I am not completely without the resource of stealth myself, Wolfingham,' the older man snapped impatiently. 'I left my home by the servants' entrance, hired a hackney cab to bring me to within two streets of this house and walked the rest of the way. All whilst keeping watch for any who might be taking any undue interest in my movements.'

'I apologise.' Darian gave a rueful inclination of his head.

'Apology accepted.' Maystone nodded briskly. 'Could we now return to the subject of these assassins and their infernal plots?'

Darian sank back into his armchair. 'I presume you are now about to tell us what part you expect the two of us to play in foiling this plot?'

Mariah had been aware of the sharpness and acuity of Wolfingham's intelligence, but she had also learnt a wary respect for his astuteness these past few minutes as the two gentlemen talked and knew, by the irritation in Aubrey Maystone's face, that the Duke's words had once again hit their mark.

'What could the two of us possibly do that you have not already done yourself?' she prompted guardedly; positively the last thing she wished for was to spend any more time in Darian Hunter's company than she needed to.

Aubrey Maystone seemed completely unaware of her reservations as his next words instantly trampled that wish. 'Mariah has already told me that she has accepted her invitation to go to Lord and Lady Nicholses' house party in Kent this weekend. I now wish for you to accompany her, Wolfingham.'

'But—'

'I am aware it is not your usual choice of entertainment, Wolfingham,' the older man acknowledged drily. 'But in this instance it is too dangerous for Mariah to attend alone.'

'Then why attend at all?' she questioned sharply, her heart having leapt in alarm just at the thought of spending a weekend in the company of the judgemental Darian Hunter. He despised her utterly already, enjoyed thinking the worst of her, without the added humiliation of knowing he was watching her with those cold green eyes as she moved about flirtatiously at one of Clara Nichols's licentious weekend house parties. 'It will be no hardship to me to send my apologies to Clara Nichols.'

'That is the last thing I wish you to do, my dear,' Aubrey Maystone assured gently, before launching into an explanation of exactly why the two of them must attend the Nicholses' house party together.

'And to think that you once told me that such things as politics and intrigue bored you,' Wolfingham drawled mockingly.

Lord Maystone, having stated his business, had now departed as abruptly as he had arrived, after stating that he would now leave the two of them alone together, so that they might discuss and consider his request, before giving him their answer later on today.

A request, as far as Mariah was concerned, that was so outrageous as to be unthinkable.

And yet…

She had never said no to anything that Aubrey Maystone had asked of her in the past and she could not bear to think of doing so now, either.

Except for the fact that this time it involved Wolfingham, a man she had serious reason to be wary of.

Her gaze flickered across to where Wolfingham now lounged in the armchair opposite her own, both the pot of tea and the decanter of brandy now empty, after almost an hour of intense discussion. 'I believe you also allowed me to continue to think that you came by your bullet wound by engaging in a duel rather than disposing of André Rousseau?'

'How delicately you put it, my dear Mariah!' Wolfingham drawled. 'But I also have reason to believe that you have greatly enjoyed tormenting *me* with the possibility of it coming about because of some tragic love affair?' He arched a mocking brow.

Yes, Mariah had indeed enjoyed taunting the haughtily disapproving Duke of Wolfingham with the possibility of his having fought a duel over a woman.

Only to now know that he had come by his bullet wound after days of secretly scouting the French countryside for information to bring back to the English government. Followed by a hand-to-hand fight in which the other man—the Frenchman André Rousseau, a spy for Napoleon, both here in England and in France—had died and Darian Hunter had been shot.

'It would seem that we have both had something to hide,' Wolfingham bit out abruptly. 'The question is, what do we do now in regard to Maystone's audacious request of the two of us?'

It *was* outrageous, Mariah acknowledged with a pained wince. Worse than outrageous, as it involved herself and Darian Hunter giving every appearance, in public at least, of being intimately involved with each other. An affair they were to use as their cover when, if, the two of them agreed to attend the house party at Lord and Lady Nicholses' house in Kent this following weekend.

Because the Nicholses had, apparently, been named in the plot against the Prince.

The Nicholses were notorious for giving licentious house parties once or twice a Season. Parties at which the Prince Regent, usually resident in a house nearby, always made an appearance on the Saturday evening of the masked ball, although Aubrey Maystone and other members of the government had succeeded in persuading the Regent into not attending this one.

The Prince Regent particularly enjoyed making an appearance at such parties as these, occasions not designed for the attendance of the young debutantes and their marriage-minded mamas, but for the older, more sophisticated members of the *ton*, where their *risqué* behaviour would not be frowned upon.

Mariah would never dream of allowing Christina to attend, for example. Having accepted her own invitation, Mariah had instantly made arrangements for her young daughter to spend the weekend at the home of her friend Diana Gilbert. Diana's mother, Lady Gilbert, intended to chaperon her own daughter and Christina to a musical soirée on Friday evening and then a ball on Saturday evening, followed by church on Sunday morning, and Mariah would return in the evening.

Mariah had always made a point of attending the Nicholses' weekend parties, when inhibitions became relaxed and information was more freely given.

A lowering of inhibitions that Mariah now accepted could—and according to Aubrey Maystone's information, had—equally have been used to Lord or Lady Nicholses' advantage.

Aubrey Maystone's suggestion was that, the danger being high, Wolfingham would now accompany Mariah into Kent, posing as her lover. Explaining that it would not be unexpected, when the two of them had been seen talking and dancing together several times this past week or so, and apparently giving rise to a certain amount of gossip and speculation concerning whether or not there might be a relationship between the two of them.

Mariah could not claim to have heard any of that unwelcome gossip herself, but then she could not expect to have done, when that gossip was about her.

It would be an easy step, Maystone had assured, for the two of them to attend the house party together and so confirm the gossip and speculation.

But it was a pretence that Mariah, despite those two occasions in which Wolfingham had held her in his arms or kissed her, would not have believed the austere and disdainful Duke of Wolfingham to be capable of.

Before today...

Mariah had no doubts now that Wolfingham had indeed chosen to hide his real self behind the guise of that cold and disdainful duke, because she now suspected—*knew*—that behind that haughty exterior was a man of deep passions.

Deep and unrelenting passions that terrified her at the same time as they caused a wild fluttering inside her.

She straightened determinedly. 'You do understand that, if I should agree to do this in order to flush out the traitors, the public liaison between the two of us would be for appearances' sake only? That there would be no actual intimacy?'

Her eyes widened as Wolfingham gave a rueful chuckle, the signs of that humour, in the warmth of his green eyes and the soft curve of chiselled lips, instantly lessening his veneer of austerity and making him appear years younger than his age.

'You do have a certain way with words, Mariah.' Darian gave a wry shake of his head. 'And I assure you, I never doubted for a moment that our liaison,' he drily echoed her own words, 'would be for appearances' sake only.' He sobered. '*If* we should agree to go forward with Maystone's proposal,' he added harshly, 'which neither of us has yet done.'

Mariah did not see how either of them had any real choice in the matter, if the perpetrators of this plot to assassinate the Prince Regent were to be arrested.

Chapter Six

'What have you done with Lady Christina this weekend?' Darian prompted as he and Mariah travelled into Kent on Friday evening in the warmth of his lamplit coach. His valet and Mariah's maid, along with their luggage, had already travelled into Kent in a second coach sent on ahead earlier today.

Cool turquoise eyes turned to look at him across the width of the coach. Mariah looked cosily warm in a travelling cloak, bonnet and muff for her hands of that same vibrant turquoise colour. 'She is staying with friends.'

'And do you trust that my younger brother will not take advantage of your absence?' Darian had sent a note informing his brother that he would be away in the country this weekend, but not with whom; he fully expected to hear of his brother's displeasure if or when Anthony learnt that Darian had spent the weekend in the company of the mother of the young lady about whom he had serious intentions.

'I trust my daughter not to allow any gentleman to take advantage of my absence.' Mariah had chosen not to speak to Christina regarding Anthony Hunter in particular, believing that to do so would only cause her independent-minded young daughter's attention to fixate on the gentleman. But a casual conversation between mother and daughter had confirmed that Christina did not have serious feelings for any of the young gentlemen who flocked to her side on every social occasion.

Wolfingham nodded. 'And Lady Nichols was receptive to my accompanying you?'

Mariah gave a dismissive snort. 'What society hostess would not be receptive to counting the elusive Duke of Wolfingham amongst her guests?'

'The Countess of Carlisle?' Darian arched a mocking brow.

'True,' that countess drawled dismissively before turning away to look out of the window into the dark of the night.

This was the first time that Darian had seen Mariah since they had informed Maystone of their decision to attend the Nicholses' weekend house party together, their arrangements having then been made through an exchange of terse notes.

A terseness that obviously still existed between the two of them now that they were together again.

Darian straightened on his side of the coach. 'And how successful do you think we shall be at this ruse of an affair between the two of us, when you cannot even bring yourself to look at me for longer than a few seconds?'

Mariah closed her eyes briefly behind the brim of her bonnet before gathering herself to once again look coolly across the carriage at Wolfingham. 'We have not arrived at Eton Park yet, your Grace.'

Darian Hunter gave a mocking shake of his head. 'It is then that I am to expect that the woman who now calls me your Grace so condescendingly will suddenly turn into my adoring lover?'

Mariah firmly repressed the shiver that ran the length of her spine—she did not care to search too deeply as to whether it was a shudder of revulsion or a quiver of anticipation!—at the mere suggestion of herself and this forcefully powerful man ever really becoming lovers.

Wolfingham was just so *immediate*. So overpoweringly male. Just so—so *Wolfingham* that he would totally possess any woman brave enough to attempt to match herself against the passions that Mariah now knew, without a doubt, burned so fiercely behind that mask of stern disapproval.

Even seated in the confines of this coach with him Mariah was aware of that fire smouldering, burning, beneath his outwardly relaxed, even bored, countenance.

'I will never be any man's adoring lover, Wolfingham,' she scorned—or any man's lover at all! 'And I will only be your *pretend* lover for this one weekend,' she assured firmly. 'I believe that you will also find my acting skills are more than sufficient as to be convincing once we are in the company of others.' How could they not be, when for years she had managed, in public at least, to look as if she found pleasure in being at her husband's side?

'And might I enquire as to where and how you might have attained and honed these acting skills?' Wolfingham arched a sceptical brow.

'Perhaps you should turn your attention to your own performance rather than worrying about mine?' she challenged sharply rather than answer his question.

Darian noted that the asperity, which usually edged Mariah's tone whenever she spoke to him, had now returned. It was an improvement on her earlier cool uninterest, but only barely!

He settled more comfortably against the plush cushions of the seat. 'I do not recall ever having received any complaints in the past regarding my performance,' he drawled mockingly.

A flush now coloured Mariah's cheeks, of either embarrassment or anger—though Darian would guess at it being the latter; there was no reason for Mariah to feel embarrassment discussing such a subject when she had been a married lady for many years and so familiar with her husband's performance. And that of the other gentlemen who had shared her bed during and after her marriage!

A thought that did not give Darian any pleasure whatsoever.

He eyed her with frustration from behind lowered lids. Indeed, it had been long days—and nights—of frustrations since the morning he had called at her home and they had been joined by Aubrey Maystone.

Not least because Mariah had proved so elusive on the occasions Darian had asked for the two of them to meet in person since that time, so that they might discuss how they were to proceed this weekend. Requests Mariah had consistently refused, on the excuse of having far too many other engagements, and the arrangements to be made for their weekend away in Kent, to be able to fit a visit from him into that busy schedule.

Darian's suggestion that, as her lover, he was *supposed* to be visiting her had been met with a wall of silence on Mariah's part. A silence that had not been broken until he had called at her home to collect her earlier this evening.

Another frustration had been Maystone's inability to persuade any of the three men, now being held and questioned, into giving them more information regarding one or both of the Nicholses' involvement in this plot against the Prince.

Thankfully, Maystone and other members of the government had succeeded in continuing to convince the Prince Regent that it was for the best that he not attend even the Nicholses' masked ball on Saturday evening.

Instead, Aubrey Maystone and several of his agents would take up residence at Winterton Manor for the weekend, just five miles away from Eton Park, and await word from Darian and Mariah as to the Nicholses' reaction to the note the Prince Regent would have delivered to them at Eton Park at precisely five o'clock on Saturday afternoon, explaining his absence. Five o'clock had been chosen deliberately, when all would be gathered for tea, so that Mariah and Darian might observe Lord and Lady Nicholses' reaction to the news, and also what followed. If anything.

It was the thought of being thrust into the midst of this weekend of licentiousness that had become yet another thorn in Darian's side, when he would normally avoid such events like the plague. Not because, as Mariah was so fond of telling him, he was too proper and austere to attend, but simply because he preferred to perform acts of intimacy without an audience. *All* acts of intimacy.

Such as the numerous acts of intimacy he had imagined engaging in with Mariah, the moment he had retired to his bed these past three nights.

Resulting in him rising early each morning following a restless night's sleep, in order to take a cold bath, before joining one or other of his friends at the boxing saloon and so allowing him to dispel some of his frustration in the boxing ring.

All of which Darian doubted would be a possible outlet for all of his restless energy during this weekend spent in Kent at Mariah's side.

No, he fully expected to be put through even

worse torture whilst in the Nicholses' home. Especially since, as was usual at these types of unrestrained weekends of entertainment, his bedchamber would no doubt tactfully adjoin Mariah's own.

Having already spent several hours in the coach with Mariah, that exotic and erotic perfume once again invading his senses, Darian was unsure whether or not he would be able to withstand the nightly temptation of opening the door that connected his bedchamber to hers.

'Do you always wear the same perfume?'

Mariah looked sharply across at Wolfingham, surprised by the sudden, and harshly spoken, change of subject, but also searching for some sign of criticism. As usual his expression proved too enigmatic for her to decipher.

Her chin rose. 'You do not like it?'

'It is unusual,' he answered noncommittally.

Mariah laughed softly. 'That does not answer my question, Wolfingham.'

'Darian.'

She blinked. 'I beg your pardon?'

'So far we have progressed from having you

address me as your Grace to the more familiar Wolfingham. I thought now might be as good a time as any for you to begin calling me Darian.'

'Did you?' Mariah returned with the coolness that had become her only defence against the fire of emotions she now knew burned behind those cold green eyes. Emotions that surprisingly sparked something similar within her own fast-beating heart.

Wolfingham now shrugged those exception-ally wide shoulders, shown to such advantage in the black fitted superfine, as was the flatness of his stomach beneath a grey waistcoat and snowy white linen, his pantaloons also black, his legs long and sprawling as he relaxed back against his side of the carriage. 'I believe most couples, in a situation such as ours is supposed to be, ad-dress each other by their given names rather than their titles.'

'You believe?' Mariah gave a taunting smile. 'Do you not know for certain?'

Darian's mouth thinned at what he knew to be her deliberate mockery. 'The ladies I have bed-ded in the past have not usually had the privilege of a title,' he drawled dismissively and had the satisfaction of seeing that blush once again colour Mariah's cheeks. 'But I have no particular aversion to addressing you at all times as Countess, if that is the game you like to play?' His brief moment of satisfaction quickly faded as he saw the smile instantly waver and then disappear from those beautiful red lips, her gaze equally as uncertain. He rose abruptly to his feet. 'Mariah—'

'Stay on your own side of the carriage, Wolfingham.' She held up a hand to ward him off from his obvious intention of crossing the carriage to sit on the seat beside her.

Darian froze even as he studied her face intently, noting the shadows beneath those beautiful eyes and the way the colour had now deserted her cheeks, leaving her pale and delicate. At thoughts of his moving closer to her? 'Are you sure you wish to go ahead with this charade, Mariah?' he finally prompted gently.

She smiled tightly. 'Who else will do it if we do not?'

He had no answer to that argument, knowing

as he did, as Mariah did, that time was not their friend. That Napoleon, having been joined by the defector Marshal Ney, and his army ever increasing, was now fast approaching Paris. There were already riots in the capitol in support of their emperor's return and King Louis was preparing to flee. If something were to now happen to England's Prince Regent, it was guaranteed to throw the allies into total disarray, so allowing Napoleon's return to the capitol to be a double-edged triumph.

Darian sank back down on to his seat, but remained sitting forward so that he might reach out and take both Mariah's hands from inside her muff, frowning as he felt the way that her fingers trembled as he held them in his own. 'There is nothing for you to be frightened of, Mariah,' he assured gruffly. 'I promise I will do my utmost to ensure that no harm shall come to you this weekend.'

Mariah held back the hysterical laugh that threatened to burst forth at the obvious sincerity of Darian's promise of allowing no harm to come to her—when the person she now feared the most was *him*.

Oh, not him exactly, but her responses to him certainly. Responses, of heat and desire, that did not seem to have dissipated or lessened in these past three days of not seeing him, as she had hoped that they might.

Responses that she had believed herself to be incapable of feeling towards any man.

Until Wolfingham.

Just a few minutes of being back in his company and Mariah had known that she was still aware of everything about him. The dark and glossy thickness of his hair. Those beautiful emerald-green eyes. The stark and chiselled handsomeness of his features. The strength of his muscled body.

The gentleness of the long and sensitive hands that now held her hands so lightly, but securely, within his own.

Hands that Mariah could only too easily imagine moving, exploring her body, lighting a fire wherever they touched, giving pleasure wherever they caressed. And what did she know of the pleasure of her body at any man's hands?

Nothing, came the blunt and unequivocal answer.

If she really were a normal widow, the woman of experience Wolfingham believed her to be, then she would know. Just as she would take every advantage of their weekend together to explore this attraction she felt for him.

Except Mariah was not normal, as a widow or a woman.

Christina had been conceived on the one and only occasion Martin had— No, Mariah could never think of what he had done to her that night as making love! It had been force and pain, and humiliation for her, nothing more and nothing less.

Their marriage had been nothing but a sham from the beginning, Martin spending most of his nights in the bed of his mistress, the same woman who acted as housekeeper in their London home, and had done so for twenty years or more before Mariah and Martin were married.

Many wives might have resented having her

husband's mistress actually living in one of their homes, but Mariah had felt only gratitude; whilst Martin's nights were occupied with Mrs Smith then he would not think of coming to her bed. She had dismissed Mrs Smith after Martin's death, of course, for Christina's sake as well as her own, but Mariah's gratitude to that lady had been such that she had provided the other woman with a large enough pension for her to live comfortably for the rest of her life.

What would Wolfingham—a man who believed her to have been an adulteress in her marriage and to have had a multitude of lovers during her five years of widowhood—what would such a man think if he were to learn that Mariah had had but a single night of carnal knowledge in her life and that one occasion had been the most horrible, degrading, painful—

'Where have you gone, Mariah?' Darian had not liked the way in which her expression had grown distant, turned inwards, her thoughts giving a shadow to the depths of those beautiful eyes. He liked it even less when she had given an obvious shudder just now of what seemed like revulsion…

Because she did genuinely fear the coming events at the Nicholses' home?

Or because she felt revulsion for the idea of even that *pretence* of an intimate relationship with him?

Unfortunately, Darian had no answer to that question.

She roused herself with effort, purposefully pulling her hands from his as she straightened, a bright and meaningless smile now curving those ruby-red lips, a smile that did nothing to take away the shadows in her eyes. 'Why, I am right here in the carriage with you, Wolfingham,' she assured him with unmistakable brittleness. 'And I do believe we are now on the driveway approaching Eton Park,' she added with obvious relief.

Darian leant back abruptly against the cushions, knowing that their brief moment of tenderness was over. If it had ever really begun on Mariah's part.

His expression was grim as he turned to look

out of the window to view the brightly lit house in the distance. He inwardly cursed himself for being a fool. He might have spent the past days and nights thinking of, desiring, Mariah, might even have anticipated being with her again, but she had shown him time and time again that she did not feel that same desire towards him.

He gave a shake of his head as he once again turned his own thoughts to the business of the weekend ahead. 'What sort of entertainments might I expect to endure this evening?'

Mariah shrugged. 'The full entertainments will not begin until tomorrow, obviously, but after dinner this evening I expect there will be cards and dancing.'

Darian grimaced. 'Sounds boringly normal to me.'

She chuckled huskily. 'I assure you there is nothing "normal" about cards and dancing in the Nicholses' home!'

Darian eyed her speculatively. 'Meaning?'

A small, secretive smile hovered at the corners of her mouth. 'You will see soon enough!'

Darian disliked the sound of that. As he disliked feeling as if he were at a disadvantage, as he surely was where such weekends as this were concerned.

And meaning that he would have to look to Mariah for guidance as to the correct way for him to behave.

But first, it seemed, he had to endure the simpering and coquettish Lady Clara Nichols as she gushingly welcomed him to her home, whilst her husband showed Mariah similar attentions. Attentions, he noted with satisfaction, that she laughed off quite easily.

Darian was not so successful where Lady Clara was concerned, as she proudly introduced them to the rest of the company still assembled in the drawing room after tea: several lords, an earl, half a dozen Members of Parliament, some with their wives, but most not. There were also a dozen or so other female members of the *ton*, a titled lady or two, several Honourables, three well-known actresses and an opera singer, and all without the escort of their husbands.

Lady Clara then insisted, her arm firmly linked

with Darian's, on personally accompanying them up the stairs to show them to their bedchambers.

Darian felt quite sickened by her attentions by the time that lady finally took herself off to rejoin her other guests and no doubt indulge in gossip about the duke and the countess.

His top lip curled with distaste the moment the door of the bedchamber had closed behind his simpering hostess. 'There is something particularly sickening about a lady of possibly forty years giggling like a schoolgirl.'

Mariah chuckled, no doubt at the look of disgust on his face, as she untied her bonnet and threw it down on to her bed. 'How very ungrateful of you, Darian, when I do believe, from their situation of being at the front of the house and the opulence of these bedchambers, that Clara and Richard must have moved out of their own bedchambers in order to accommodate the two of us.'

As expected, the two of them had been given adjoining bedchambers, the door between those rooms having been left pointedly open, and no doubt the reason Darian had been subjected to

Clara Nichols's girlishly suggestive giggles when she reminded them that dinner would be served in a little over two hours. No doubt she expected the two of them to indulge in some love play before that time.

Darian's room was acceptable, but Mariah's—Clara Nichols's own bedchamber?—was a ghastly nightmare of pink and cream lace and flounces. 'How will you ever be able to sleep in such an explosion of pink?' He grimaced as he stood in the doorway between their two rooms.

Mariah gave a dismissive shrug. 'I shall simply blow out the candles and then I shall not be able to see it.'

Darian admired the picture of grace and beauty Mariah made in the candle and firelight as she stood in the middle of that ghastly pink room. A veritable vision in turquoise and cream, her hair appearing like spun gold, colour now warming her cheeks.

His blood stirred and he felt that tingling at the base of his spine and between his thighs, the rising and thickening of his erection, as he imagined how much more lovely Mariah would look without any clothes on at all.

Would the curls between her thighs be that same gold or possibly a shade darker?

Would her nipples be the same ruby red as her lips?

And would the folds between her thighs—

'If you would not mind, Darian?' Mariah's voice softly interrupted his erotic musings. 'My maid will be here shortly to help me bathe and dress for dinner, as no doubt will your own valet. Oh, and, Darian…?' she added as he gave a terse bow of acceptance before turning to leave, waiting until he had slowly turned back to her before speaking again. 'Close the door on your way out, please.'

His jaw tightened at the dismissal as he stepped through the doorway and closed the door behind him, knowing he needed the privacy in order to take care of the need throbbing through his body, before he dared to rejoin Mariah!

'You are not intending to appear in that gown in public!'

Mariah turned from where she had been gazing at her reflection in the mirror as she put the last of the pearl clips into her hair, to now look at Wolfingham as he once again stood in the open doorway between their two bedchambers. His appearance was as resplendent as usual in black evening clothes and snowy white linen, an ebony sheen to his hair, his features once again as hard as granite.

It was the look of horror on those hard features, as he gazed back at her unblinkingly, that now brought a wry smile to her lips. 'You do not like it?'

Like it? Darian had never seen a gown like it before! Well, not outside the walls of a brothel, at least.

The gown left Mariah's shoulders bare except for two tiny ribbon straps and was made of some diaphanous cream material, lined with the sheerest of lace. It clearly revealed the bare outline of the curvaceous body beneath and darkening at the apex between Mariah's thighs—revealing the nakedness of the darker curls covering her mound.

As for the bodice of the gown! It was almost non-existent, just that cream diaphanous material covering the fullness of Mariah's breasts, the nipples plump berries and clearly showing through as being as ruby red as her lips—that ruby colour aided by rouge, if he was not mistaken.

His traitorous body had surged back into full attention the moment he looked at the reflection of those plump nipples in the mirror, and imagined Mariah applying that rouge to those succulent berries. 'I see that a certain part of you does, at least.' Mariah looked pointedly at the unmistakable evidence of his arousal.

Darian did not in the least enjoy feeling like a callow youth taking his first look at a naked woman.

Except Mariah was not naked.

Perhaps he would not have reacted so strongly if she had been!

Of course he would, Darian instantly chastised himself. It was only that there was something so provocative about the tantalising glimpses of those slender and obviously naked curves as Mariah moved across the room to collect her gloves from the bed, giving just the hint of those golden curls nestling between her thighs. And her breasts were magnificent; creamy, full and plump, with those red and succulent rouged nipples just begging to be tasted and suckled.

Darian wanted nothing more at that moment than to lay Mariah down upon the bed before taking those berries into his mouth and sucking and tasting their plumpness until he was sated.

If he ever was!

As for the shadow of those darker golden curls and the promise of what lay hidden between her thighs—

Darian imagined lowering her gently down on to the bed and pushing her gown up her thighs so that he might explore every silken inch of that hidden treasure. To caress the plumpness of her folds. Taste and suck the tiny nubbin above—

Beads of perspiration broke out on Darian's forehead as he fought an inward battle not to give in to the urge to cross the room and take Mariah in his arms, to fulfil every single one of the fantasies that had been slowly driving him insane and that he now found impossible to stop.

'I am ready to go downstairs and join the other guests, if you are?'

It took every effort of his indomitable will to pull Darian back from the brink of giving in to his desires, his voice harsh as he answered her. 'Do you have a shawl or something you can wear about your shoulders?' The thought of other men ogling Mariah's almost naked breasts, and that tantalising outline of her naked curves beneath her gown, was enough to make him clench his fists violently.

Mariah gave a bell-like laugh as she collected up a fan from her dressing table rather than a shawl. 'You will see, Darian, my gown is quite modest in comparison with the gowns some of the other ladies will be wearing this evening.'

He had no interest in what the other ladies were wearing this evening; they could all walk around stark naked for all Darian cared. But if he caught one single gentleman in the act of ogling Mariah— He was behaving more than ridiculously, Darian recognised self-disgustedly, when he had no more right to approve or disapprove of other gentlemen ogling Mariah, tonight or any other night, than—than the Prince Regent did!

Although he had no doubt that the Prince Regent, if he had been one of the guests this evening, would have taken great delight in enjoying Mariah's appearance. The man might be plumper and more dissipated than he had been in his youth, but he still had charm enough to seduce the ladies.

Whereas Darian's charm, what little he did possess—and no doubt Mariah would say he possessed none!—seemed to have completely deserted him for the moment.

'Darian?' Mariah prompted again lightly.

He gathered himself to straighten determinedly before crossing the room to hold out his arm to her, feeling much as he had when he had necessarily to prepare himself before a battle.

And unsure whether that battle this evening would be with his own wayward emotions, or with the other gentlemen present.

Chapter Seven

Mariah was enjoying herself.

Actually enjoying herself, when normally she would simply have gone through the motions of doing so at this sort of entertainment, flirting and laughing with the gentlemen whilst at the same time keeping them in line—and their groping hands firmly at bay—with a delicately aimed flick of her fan.

And the reason she was enjoying herself was standing broodingly at her side now that all the guests had retired to the drawing room following dinner, giving every appearance of a dark and avenging angel, ready to swoop down on any who might even think of crossing over the invisible line he had drawn about the two of them since they had sat down to dinner earlier.

The dark and avenging angel Darian Hunter, the Duke of Wolfingham.

As she had warned Wolfingham before coming down the stairs earlier, most of the other ladies were dressed much more daringly than she was this evening. Indeed, there was a plethora of completely bared breasts visible about the drawing room as the gentlemen, and many of the ladies, completely against the normal rules of polite society, enjoyed an after-dinner brandy together. Most of the gowns were without the benefit of that layer of lace that covered Mariah's breasts and several of the gowns were made of a totally transparent and gauzy material that left absolutely nothing to the imagination.

And for all the notice Wolfingham had taken— was still taking!—of any of those erotically displayed ladies, they might as well have been wearing sackcloth.

It was a refreshing change for Mariah to be in the presence of a gentleman whose gaze was not constantly wandering to the half-naked bodies of other women.

Just as Wolfingham's glowering and tight-lipped disapproval of the approach of both the ladies and the gentlemen present this evening had kept everyone but their hostess from attempting to interrupt their privacy. Wolfingham had wasted no time in dispatching that lady, too, with a few choice and tersely spoken words.

Instead, he had centred all of his attention on Mariah as they ate the sumptuously prepared dinner served to them earlier, his conversation exclusive, and occasionally feeding her the odd delicacy of food from his own plate, as a way, no doubt, of giving further illusion to their intimacy.

Mariah had blushed like a schoolgirl the first time Darian behaved so unexpectedly, that blush having deepened as he centred his hawklike gaze upon her lips when she finally leant forward to take the food from his fork. She had been better prepared the second time it had happened, but still felt unaccountably hot at the way his green gaze stared so intently at her lips.

And throughout all of it Darian had seemed completely unaware of the sexual play going on about them.

The assembled company had been slightly

restrained to begin with, all obviously aware of having the imposing Duke of Wolfingham within their midst, but several glasses of wine later, along with Wolfingham's apparent distraction with Mariah, and those inhibitions had quickly fallen away.

Several of the gentlemen had openly caressed and tweaked bared breasts, and one gentleman had even crawled beneath the table for several minutes, the expression of rapture on the flushed face of the actress seated next to him, followed by her breathy and noisy gasps of pleasure as she climaxed, clearly showing where that gentleman was lavishing his attentions.

Mariah had glanced away as if bored as the gentleman crawled back up into his seat, his mouth moist and lips swollen, the expression on his flushed face becoming one of equal rapture as that lady returned the favour, by unbuttoning his pantaloons and openly stroking him until he, too, reached a completion.

It was a disgusting and embarrassing display, and one that Mariah had been forced to witness at least a dozen times during these past seven years of spying for the Crown.

And one that tonight had caused a flush of heat to course through Mariah's own veins and an unaccustomed tingling and warmth to spread between her thighs.

A heat and tingling that she had preferred not to question too deeply.

'Say no, Darian,' she warned Wolfingham softly now as she shook her own head at Clara Nichols as the other woman moved about the room gathering up the people who wished to play cards.

Darian gave a terse shake of his own head to their poutingly disappointed hostess before moving to stand slightly in front of Mariah, the broadness of his back and shoulders blocking her from the view of the majority of the other guests in the room. 'Why?' he returned as softly.

Mariah looked up at him beneath lowered lashes. 'Because I doubt you will like the forfeit if you lose. Do you ever lose?'

Darian raised one dark brow. 'At cards?'

'At anything!'

Well, he was certainly losing his battle tonight in regard to the desire he felt for Mariah.

Dinner with the Nicholses' guests had been a disgusting display of body parts and licentious behaviour, which he had found distinctly untitillating and which had actually turned his stomach on several occasions. Several sexual acts had actually occurred at the dinner table, made all the more incongruous by the fact that they were all seated about a formal dining table in an equally formal dining room and were being waited upon by the Nicholses' placid-faced butler and footmen.

He had noticed several gentlemen eyeing Mariah covetously when they first sat down at the dinner table. Glances he had frowned darkly upon. Those glances had then turned towards Darian, envious in some cases and actually belligerent in one or two others.

Because none of those gentlemen had been numbered amongst Mariah's lovers? Darian hoped it was so.

He had soon forgotten all but Mariah, as he shut out the presence and behaviour of the people around them and concentrated all of his attentions on her.

He had enjoyed talking with her, their conversations intelligent and witty. He had also fed her sweetmeats on occasion, initially as a way of publically demonstrating the intimacy of their relationship, but continuing to do so time and time again as his shaft hardened as he watched her lips encircle his fork and imagined how those soft and full lips would feel encircling him in the same sensuous way. He had almost come undone completely when she had once run her tongue along her bottom lip as she licked away an excess of cream from a bonbon he had just fed her.

'Very rarely,' he answered her drily now. 'What exactly is it that you forfeit here for losing at cards?'

'Watch.' She turned to where two tables had now been set up with four card players on each, two gentleman and two ladies on one and three gentlemen and one lady on the other.

'Good gracious.' Darian gave a shudder just seconds later as Clara Nichols, obviously the loser of the first hand of cards, instantly stood up to remove her gown, resuming her seat dressed only in silk drawers and pale stockings held up by two pink—what other colour would the woman choose!—garters, her breasts hanging down like two giant udders. 'There should be a law against such an unpleasant display.' Darian's mouth twisted with distaste.

'No doubt there is outside of the privacy of one's home.' Mariah smiled up at him impishly. 'And some gentlemen find such full breasts… erotic.'

'I cannot see how they could!'

'Watch,' she encouraged again, just in time for Darian to glance across the room and see a prominent member of the government—prominent in more ways than one at this precise moment!—lying back upon Lady Clara's bare thighs and placing his head beneath one of her pendulous breasts before sucking the nipple heartily into his mouth.

'He looks like a giant baby taking suck from its mother!' Darian muttered with disgust.

'I believe that is Lord Edgewood's little fetish, yes.' Mariah nodded. 'And many women's breasts become less pert as we age, especially when we have borne children,' she added with a playful tap of her fan on his shoulder.

Whether intended or not—and Darian suspected not, in his particular case—the movement drew attention to her own perfectly formed and jiggling breasts, beautifully pert rouge-tipped breasts that peeped out at him temptingly from beneath that thin barrier of lace. 'I am pleased to note your own have not suffered from a similar malaise,' he murmured gruffly.

Mariah's breath caught in her throat, her eyes widening in alarm, as she realised she had actually been *flirting* with Darian Hunter, the imposing and disapproving Duke of Wolfingham, these past few minutes. Openly, coquettishly, *flirting*.

'I believe I have seen quite enough for one evening,' Wolfingham now muttered harshly as he turned away as one of the gentlemen on the second card table, a short and overly plump member of the aristocracy, stood up to remove his trousers, revealing his small and glistening manhood sticking out from the opening of his smallclothes. 'Shall we retire?' He held out his arm to Mariah, a nerve pulsing in the hardness of his cheek.

She raised teasing brows as she rested her gloved hand lightly upon his arm and allowed him to accompany her from the room, aware of several pairs of eyes following their abrupt departure. 'You do realise that everyone will assume we are going upstairs for the sole purpose of making love together?' she teased drily as Wolfingham took a lighted candle from the butler before they ascended the staircase together.

'Let them think it!' Darian doubted he had ever actually made love to any woman. Had sex with, yes, but never made love with or to.

But this evening—*that* had been nothing more than several hours of a sickening display of unrestrained debauchery and was beyond enduring for even another moment.

He gave a shudder as they came to a halt as they reached the top of the staircase. 'I do believe that just the memory of that image of Clara Nichols's pendulous breasts will make it difficult for me ever to be able to become aroused again, let alone have sexual relations with a woman. I dread to think what outrageous entertainments they will think of for the masked ball tomorrow evening!'

Mariah cursed the blush that had warmed her cheeks as Wolfingham talked so frankly of his arousal. She was a widow aged four and thirty, had been a married woman for twelve of those years. And Wolfingham, along with many others, believed her to have first been an adulteress, then a mistress several times over these past five years. Women as sophisticated and experienced as Mariah Beecham was reputed to be did not blush like a schoolgirl when a man talked of his arousal.

'This is just a small house party—the majority of the guests will arrive tomorrow evening just for the ball,' she dismissed lightly. 'This evening's guests will no doubt sleep most of the day away after tonight's excesses.'

'One blessing, I suppose,' he muttered.

Mariah nodded. 'I am afraid the wearing of masks tomorrow evening allows for even more licentious behaviour than you have witnessed this evening. Also, the Nicholses' smaller and private ballroom is…well, perhaps I should leave that as a surprise for you for tomorrow evening.'

He gave another shudder. 'I would rather you did not!'

Mariah was about to answer him when there came the sound of loud shouts and whistles of approval from down the stairs. 'I do believe another lady or gentleman has just been divested of another article of clothing.'

Wolfingham looked frostily down the long length of his nose. 'In that case I see little reason to celebrate.' He drew in a deep breath. 'Please tell me that you have never— Assure me that none of those *gentlemen* have ever—'

'No,' Mariah assured him hastily, the warmth deepening in her cheeks.

Those green eyes narrowed. 'None of them?'

Mariah's jaw tightened. 'No.'

'There is a God, after all!' he rasped with feeling as he took hold of her arm, the candle in his other hand lighting their way as they began walking down the hallway to their bedchambers.

Mariah eyed him quizzically. 'I fail to see why it should matter to you one way or the other.'

'It matters!' he ground out between clenched teeth.

'As I said, I do not see why. This, what is supposed to be between the two of us, is merely play—' The breath was knocked from Mariah's lungs as she suddenly found herself thrust up against the wall, the candle placed on a small side table as an ominous-looking Wolfingham towered over her. He had placed his hands on the wall either side of her head, making her a prisoner of both his encircling arms and the lean and muscled strength of his body. 'Darian…?' She looked up at him uncertainly between long, thick lashes.

Darian was breathing deeply, in an effort to retain his control. He had already been enraged, just at the thought of Mariah having ever been intimate with any of the other men present this weekend—he refused to think of any of those men again as ever being *gentlemen*! But being dismissed by Mariah, as if he were of no more importance to her, that he was no better than any of them, was beyond endurance.

His nostrils flared as he looked down at her between hooded lids, his senses aflame, flooded, *filled*, with both the sight of her and the increasing smell of that insidious and arousing perfume.

Her eyes were a deep and drowning turquoise, her skin creamy smooth, with that becoming blush to her cheeks. Her parted lips were so plump and tempting! The bareness of her shoulders made him ache to touch them, the hollows of her throat begging further investigation, with his lips and tongue. And her breasts moved, swelled enticingly beneath that thin lace barrier, as she breathed shallowly.

And all the time Darian gazed down at her hungrily, the very air about them seeming to have stilled, the intensity of that erotic perfume having deepened and swelled, engulfing him, *enslaving* him and threatening to destroy his last shreds of resistance.

Why had her perfume deepened now? How was it possible?

'Mariah, do you stroke your perfume across

and between your breasts and between your thighs?' he prompted gruffly.

'Darian!' she gasped breathlessly.

'Do you?' he pressed raggedly.

'I— Yes. Yes!' she confirmed achingly.

And telling Darian that, for the perfume to have become stronger, Mariah's body heat must have deepened, and so increasing the perfume escaping from those secret, hot places.

He closed his eyes briefly, hoping it might aid him in holding on to his fast-slipping control. But closing his eyes only intensified his sensitivity to her perfume. He slowly opened half-raised lids, his heated gaze immediately homing in on the soft pout of Mariah's parted lips. Lips he had been longing to taste again since she climbed into his carriage earlier today.

An ache he found he could no longer resist as he held her gaze with his own, his arms on the wall beside her keeping his body from touching hers, as he slowly lowered his head to run his lips lightly across her slightly parted ones.

They were soft and hesitant beneath his own, tasting of sweetmeats and brandy as he ran his tongue gently along and between them, running lightly across the ridge of her teeth, stroking along the moist length of her own tongue, before retreating to start the caress all over again, their ragged breathing becoming hot and humid between them.

Mariah had never been kissed so gently before, so slowly and so *erotically*, her pulse leaping, and her heart beating loudly beneath breasts that had become swollen and sensitised, just the gentle brush of that lace across them causing her nipples to harden and ache as they became engorged and swollen almost to the point of pain. Just as she was aware of a similar swelling, heat, between her thighs.

Her neck arched as Darian's lips now travelled across her cheek, teeth nibbling her earlobe before moving lower still. Her hands moved out to grasp Darian's shoulders as she felt his lips against her throat, gently sucking on that flesh, tongue lathing moistly to ease the pain before moving lower still, the brush of that hot and moist tongue now dipping into the deep and sensitive hollows at the base of her arched throat.

'Darian!' Mariah was so beset with new and unfamiliar emotions that she had no idea whether her gasp was one of protest for him to stop, or a plea for him to continue.

The response and heat of her body felt so strange to her. Not an unpleasant strange—far from it! She had never felt such pleasure before, or this deep and yearning ache she had to press closer against Darian's body, to rub herself against him, in an effort—a plea—to find relief for this hot and burning need, both in her breasts and between her thighs.

She groaned low in her throat, her knees threatening to buckle beneath her as Darian's lips and stroking tongue now explored the tops of her creamy breasts. Sighing her pleasure as she at last felt the heavy weight of Darian's thighs against her own as he leant inwards to prevent her fall, allowing her to feel his own long and engorged arousal pressed against her softness— and giving instant lie to his earlier claim!

Mariah should have felt trapped, should have felt awash with the usual panic she suffered whenever a man attempted to touch or kiss her. That need she always felt to escape. To free herself.

And yet she felt none of that with Darian, wanted only to press herself closer still, to rub herself over and against him, anything to be able to somehow alleviate the burning ache in her breasts and between her thighs.

'Darian!' Mariah gave a helpless gasp as she felt the moist stroke of his tongue across her bared nipple, the first indication she had that he had pulled down that delicate lace barrier and bared her breasts.

That stroke of his tongue was quickly followed by the hot and deliberate brush of his breath over the sensitised tip. The stroking of his tongue again, followed by that soft breath, her nipple standing erect and begging for more as he moved to lavish that same attention to its twin.

It was pleasure like nothing Mariah had ever known before, had never guessed existed.

'After you for a taste, if you don't mind, Wolfingham?'

Mariah had frozen at the first sound of that intrusive voice. She now turned her head quickly, her gaze stricken as she saw Lord Richard Nichols standing just feet away down the hallway, his face flushed with arousal, eyes fevered as he gazed unabashedly at Mariah's completely bared breasts.

That fevered gaze remained fixed lasciviously on her bared breasts as he took a step forward. 'I've long wanted a taste of this particular beauty.'

Mariah was barely aware of Wolfingham moving, aware only of the loss of his heat pressed against her as he strode ominously down the hallway towards the other man, allowing her time to pull the lace quickly back in place before looking up again as she heard Richard Nichols's squeak of protest and seeing that Darian now had the older man pressed up against the wall of the hallway, Nichols's feet dangling as he was held several inches above the floor by Wolfingham's hand about his throat. Darian's expression was one of cold fury as he looked at the other man.

'I do mind, as it happens, Nichols!' he grated harshly. 'In fact, I would mind very much if I were ever to learn that you had come within six feet of touching Mariah.'

'But—'

'Do I make myself clear?'

'Very—very clear.' The other man appeared to be having trouble breathing, let alone speaking. 'L-leave off, do, Wolfingham!' Nichols choked out, his hand about the younger man's wrist as he struggled to free himself.

Darian gazed contemptuously at Richard Nichols for several long seconds more, his gaze glacial as he conveyed a stronger, more silent threat to the older man. One of violence and retribution such as Nichols had never seen before.

'Darian?'

He was so angry, so filled with a need to shake the older man like a rag doll, like the insufferable cur that he was, that for several long moments Darian could think of nothing but the desire he felt to beat this man to within an inch of his life. He was so angry that he could not respond to Mariah's pleading.

'Darian, please!'

He heard the sob in Mariah's voice this time,

causing him to break his murderous gaze away from Nichols in order to turn and look at her. She looked so pale, so tiny and vulnerable, in the softness of the candlelight, her shadowed gaze holding his with that same pleading he had detected in her voice.

His expression softened slightly as he continued to look at her. 'Do not worry, Mariah, I do not intend to kill Nichols. Not this time,' he added harshly as he turned back to look challengingly at the other man.

His reassurance did nothing to alleviate Nichols's obvious panic, the other man's face having become an unpleasant puce colour—much like the unpleasant colour of his wife's bedchamber!—his pale eyes bulging.

Perhaps because Darian still had his hand about his throat!

Darian gave a disgusted snort as he removed his hand before taking a step back, uncaring as the other man lost his balance and almost fell to his knees as he dropped those several inches back down to the floor. 'I advise that you stay away from Mariah in future, if you know what is good for you.'

Richard Nichols had his hand raised to his bruised throat, his expression one of belligerent irritation. 'You only had to say no, old chap. There's no need for—for such violence. There is plenty to go round—' He broke off as he obviously saw the savagery of Darian's expression. 'I— Well— Yes. I think I will go and rejoin my other guests down the stairs.'

At any other time Mariah might have found amusement in seeing the indignity of the obnoxious Richard Nichols scuttling hastily down the hallway before quickly turning the corner and disappearing in the direction of the staircase.

Here and now, the older man having stood witness to the heated lovemaking between Mariah and Darian—and who knew how long he had stood observing the two of them before he spoke up!—Mariah was too upset to be able to find any amusement in the situation.

Instead, she felt humiliated and sickened, the pleasure of that lovemaking becoming as degrading as the rest of this evening's events had

202 *Darian Hunter: Duke of Desire*

been. She shuddered just thinking of Richard Nichols having lasciviously watched as Darian suckled and pleasured her breasts. Having heard her gasps and moans as the heat coursed through her body. It was— Her gaze sharpened on Wolfingham as she realised he had made no move since he had stepped back after releasing Nichols, those icy green eyes now narrowed in concentrated thought. 'What is it, Darian?' she prompted abruptly.

He drew in a deep breath before answering her distractedly. 'What was Nichols doing wandering about up here in the first place when the entertainment is downstairs?'

She gave a dismissive shrug. 'Perhaps he came to collect something?'

'Or perhaps he came up here for another reason entirely!' Darian rasped as he turned and strode determinedly down the hallway towards her, collecting up the candle and taking a firm grasp of her arm before continuing on his way to their bedchambers.

'Darian?' Mariah was totally at a loss to know what was bothering him as he stepped aside and waited for her to enter her bedchamber ahead of him, before following her inside and closing the door firmly behind him. Because something most assuredly was.

For herself, she could imagine nothing more humiliating than the two of them, their lovemaking, now being the amusing topic of conversation down the stairs, when no doubt Richard Nichols would skip over his cowardly response to Wolfingham's violent reaction, but enlarge and embellish what he had observed, for the lascivious pleasure of his listeners. It was—

'What are you doing?' She frowned as she watched Darian now moving about her bedchamber, lighting several more candles before he commenced prowling about the room. His expression was grim as he moved several paintings aside before moving on to examine the four-poster bed, stepping up on to the pink bedspread to examine the top and back of it. 'Darian?'

Angry colour stood out in the hardness of his cheeks when he finally stepped down from the bed, a nerve pulsing in his tightly clenched jaw. 'There are peepholes, through several of the paintings and the frame at the back of the bed, all neatly disguised so that none would know if not aware of them, but there nonetheless.'

'Peepholes?' Mariah repeated uncomprehendingly.

'You had no idea they were there?'

'I—' She gave a dazed shake of her head. 'I do not even know what they are.'

He grimaced. 'No doubt Nichols came up the stairs just now to check on which bedchamber we had gone into, yours or my own. His intention then being to go back down the stairs and invite his guests to come up here and observe the two of us together through those peepholes, no doubt accessed through a shallow passage between the walls.'

Mariah dropped weakly down on to the side of the bed and felt all the colour leach from her cheeks as she took in the full import of what Darian was saying to her.

A peep show. They were to have been nothing more than a—

'It did not happen, Mariah,' Darian soothed as he moved to sit on the bed beside her before taking her into his arms as she collapsed weakly against his chest; one look at the blank shock on Mariah's deathly white face had been enough to tell him that this was the first she had known of those strategically placed peepholes in the walls of Lady Nichols's bedchamber.

He felt ashamed now for having harboured even the briefest of doubts that Mariah might have been a willing participant in the entertainment the Nichols had now intended providing for their guests.

An understandable doubt, perhaps, in view of Mariah's reputation, but Darian now felt a heady relief at realising, from her collapse against him, that if they had made love together she would have been as innocently unaware of the people watching as he was.

A reputation Darian had already started to question earlier this evening and about which he now had serious doubts.

She had been at deep pains in his carriage earlier to ensure that he understood that any show of intimacy between the two of them was for show only.

The gown she wore this evening was positively virginal in comparison with the other ladies' attire.

Mariah had seemed relieved rather than disappointed when his glowering presence beside her had kept all other gentlemen at bay this evening.

She had been as disgusted as he by the sexual play they had witnessed during dinner and since.

Lastly, he would swear that her responses just now, to his kisses and the caress of his hands, lips and tongue, had been completely without guile or pretence.

As had her dismay when she realised that Richard Nichols had been watching them.

'It could have,' she choked now. 'It could have!'

Mariah pulled out of Wolfingham's arms before standing up abruptly, knowing, that if Richard Nichols had not played his hand too early, that she had been on the brink—the very brink!—of allowing her emotions to rule her head.

She had *wanted* Darian Hunter to make love to her.

She had *hungered* for it.

Had been so lost to the pleasure of his hands

and mouth, of wanting that pleasure to continue, that she had almost been on the point of *begging* him to make love to her!

It was incomprehensible.

Unbelievable.

Unacceptable!

She did not find pleasure in a man's arms, in his closeness, in his lovemaking. She never had. She never would. How could she when the single memory of that act was of the violation of her body rather than pleasure?

When Martin Beecham, the man who had later become her husband, had forced himself upon her shortly before her seventeenth birthday.

A rape of her body and her soul of which Christina was the result, thus forcing Mariah into becoming Martin's wife.

Chapter Eight

'What is it, Mariah?' Darian questioned sharply as he stood up.

He made no move to touch her again; Mariah now looked so fragile, in her emotions as well as her body, that he feared she might crumple and fall at his feet if he attempted to place so much as a finger upon her.

'You can ask me that?' she choked out incredulously, those turquoise eyes glittering brightly in the pallor of her face. 'After learning that the two of us were to be nothing more than exhibits in the Nicholses' peep show?'

He grimaced. 'Only if we had proceeded to make love together. Which we have not.'

Mariah could no longer meet his gaze. 'That does nothing to change the fact— Oh! Do you think anyone could have been behind those walls earlier this evening?' she gasped, eyes wide as she twisted her gloved fingers together.

Darian shrugged. 'I doubt, with the responsibility of his other guests, that Nichols would have found the time to come up the stairs and observe you dressing.'

'I was referring to our conversation, Darian! Did we say anything in this room earlier that might have— Do you seriously think that weasel Nichols might have *watched* me bathing and dressing earlier this evening?' Mariah's face had taken on a sickly green hue at the thought of it.

'As I recall, our conversation was perfectly innocuous earlier,' he reassured. 'I also think it more likely that Lady Nichols, after escorting us to our bedchambers, would have lingered upstairs to observe *me*!' Darian's mouth twisted with distaste for the very idea of having that pale blue gaze moving lasciviously over his naked body whilst he'd bathed and dressed earlier.

Mariah stilled. 'You believe there to be similar peepholes in your own bedchamber? In *all* the bedchambers?' she added aghast.

'After tonight I believe the master and mistress of this house to be capable of anything! After all, this is not the Nicholses' main country residence.' He shrugged. 'They do not bring their children here, for example, but leave them at their Norfolk estate with their nurse. Thank heavens for small mercies!'

Mariah thought of the other occasions when she had stayed in this house, totally unaware of the eyes that might have been secretly watching her. As she bathed. As she went about her *toilette*. As she stood completely naked before dressing.

She felt ill.

Unclean.

Violated!

As violated as she had been that night eighteen years ago when Martin had lured her into one of the private rooms at a ball they were both attending, locked the door behind them and then coldly and calculatedly assaulted her. Warning her after the event that no one would believe the word of the daughter of a minor landowner and merchant against an earl's, if she were to accuse him of the deed.

Mariah had been but sixteen years old and was too frightened, too devastated, felt too unclean, to dare take the risk of telling anyone what Martin Beecham, the Earl of Carlisle, had done to her.

Most especially so as he had also warned her that he would repeat the violation, again, and then again, until such time as she was with child. Not because he particularly wished for an heir, but so that she was forced into marrying him, thus bringing a good portion of her father's fortune into the marriage.

And it had all worked out perfectly for Martin, of course, because Mariah had become pregnant with that very first attempt. She had tried to tell her parents the truth then, but as promised, Martin had denied her accusation of his having forced her, claiming that she had been as eager as he for the coupling. He also insisted that she was merely frightened of the repercussions after the event, now that she found herself with child.

Repercussions that would cease to exist when she accepted his offer of marriage.

Whether or not her parents had believed Mariah's version of events had not mattered at this point, although she liked to think that they had; she was an only child and their relationship had always been a close one.

But whether they believed her or not, her mother and father had been left with no more choice in the matter than Mariah. She would have to accept the earl's offer of marriage. A babe born seven months after the wedding could be overlooked by society and very often was! But if Mariah refused to marry the father of her child—the more-than-willing father!—then she would be ruined and both she and her parents ostracised from society.

Faced with those choices there had been only one decision that Mariah could make.

Marriage to the very man who had raped her.

Her body might not have been violated tonight, but her privacy, her very person, had.

She was no longer a girl of sixteen, of course, too frightened to accuse the person responsible for that violation. But the reputation she had nurtured in society, as the sophisticated and flirtatious Countess of Carlisle, would most certainly be in danger if she were to now voice her complaints to her host and hostess.

As her obvious shock now had already placed that reputation in danger in regard to Darian Hunter, the astute and intelligent Duke of Wolfingham.

Mariah drew in a deep breath before straightening her shoulders and unclasping her fingers, her chin high as she turned to give Wolfingham a derisive smile. 'How unfortunate, for the Nichols, that you grew wise to their little scheme!'

Darian was relieved to see that some of the colour had now returned to Mariah's cheeks. Although he did not believe for a moment that she was as composed as she now wished to appear; her obvious shock a few minutes ago had most certainly been genuine.

A shock he might not have expected from one as promiscuous as Mariah Beecham was reputed to be.

He also wondered what thoughts had been

going through her head just a few minutes ago. Whatever they were, they had brought a grey tinge to her already pale cheeks and haunted shadows to those beautiful eyes.

'Very unfortunate,' he echoed drily, prepared, for the moment, to accept that Mariah was determined to place those walls back about her emotions. This was not the time, and certainly not the place, to question her further on the subject.

But the very fact that she had not as yet upbraided him for their lovemaking earlier was surely evidence of her inner unease?

A lovemaking, and Mariah's response, that Darian knew was going to haunt and disturb his own rest tonight—again!

'Do you have any shawls or handkerchiefs with you? I could place them over the pictures and the head of the bed to ensure your privacy,' he explained at her questioning frown.

'Oh. Oh, yes, of course,' she breathed in obvious relief as she moved to open the wardrobe and look through the things on the shelves in there. 'Here.' She handed Darian several handkerchiefs and two shawls. 'Will they be enough to prevent anyone from at least seeing into this room?'

'Oh, yes.' Darian tied the two shawls securely to the paintings before moving on to do the same to the bed with the handkerchiefs. 'There.' He nodded his satisfaction as he stepped back.

'What of your own bedchamber?'

'I have some handkerchiefs of my own,' he dismissed.

'I— Then I will wish you a good night.'

He frowned. 'Mariah—'

'I believe we have provided enough of a display for our audience for one night, Wolfingham. Besides which, it is late and I am very tired.' She arched one pointed brow.

Darian knew himself well and truly dismissed, without either of them having made direct reference to their heated lovemaking earlier.

If Nichols had not interrupted them then Darian might not have left this bedchamber at all tonight.

But equally, if Nichols had not interrupted the two of them, allowing Darian the time to think of what the other man was doing there at all, then they might even now be providing entertainment for the other guests.

Not that Darian was the prude Mariah had once thought him. Far from it. He had spent his share of time in gaming hells and the houses of the *demi-monde*, and knew full well the games played in such establishments. But that play was at the consent of both parties, not the intrusion, the violation, tonight's game would have been to the privacy of their lovemaking. He did not perform for the entertainment of strangers.

'Very well, Mariah.' He nodded as he strode across the room to bend down and kiss her lightly upon her brow. 'I wish you a good night,' he added huskily as he looked down at her intently.

Mariah felt flustered by Darian's close proximity, coming so soon after this shocking discovery of the peepholes in her bedchamber.

So soon after she had felt those strange and wonderful sensations as he made love to her earlier out in the hallway.

Sensations Mariah could still feel, in the tingling fullness of her breasts and the swollen dampness between her thighs.

And so reminiscent of those sensations she had felt when he'd kissed her at Lady Stockton's ball.

Was it possible, after all these years of feeling nothing, that her body was actually awakening to sexual arousal?

A sexual arousal caused solely and completely by Darian Hunter, the Duke of Wolfingham?

And felt only for him?

Mariah stepped back abruptly, too alarmed by even the possibility of that being true to be able to suffer his close proximity a moment longer. 'Goodnight, Wolfingham,' she stated firmly.

Darian studied her from between narrowed lids for several seconds longer, knowing from the determined set of Mariah's mouth and chin that she considered this conversation over.

He gave a terse nod. 'If you should need me, you know where I am.'

Her brows rose. 'You are suggesting that I might possibly be overcome with lust for you in the middle of the night?'

Darian grimaced at her scathingly derisive tone. 'I am suggesting that I noticed there is no key in the lock to this bedchamber. We could place a chair beneath the door handle,' he suggested as he saw the alarmed look Mariah gave in the direction of the door.

'Yes! Yes, please do,' she confirmed more coolly. 'Thank you,' she added softly, eyes downcast, as Darian saw to the placing of that chair.

Darian sighed his frustration as he looked at her bent head for several seconds more. Not sexual frustration—that seemed to be with him constantly whenever he was with Mariah. And when he was not!

No, his frustration now was due to another reason entirely.

With Mariah he so often felt as if he took one step forward and then was forced, by circumstances, into taking two steps back. As now. Their lovemaking had been beyond enjoyable. Darian could not remember ever having been aroused quite so quickly, or so strongly, by any other woman. And he knew, from the obvious responses of her body, her breathless sighs of pleasure, that Mariah had been just as aroused. And yet now she was dismissing him as if that closeness had never happened.

It was beyond frustrating; it was infuriating.

Mariah was a woman of four and thirty, had been a married woman for twelve of those years, and as such she could not be unaware of how much he had wanted to make love to and with her a short time ago. Or that she returned that desire for him to make love to and with her. And yet she behaved now as if that desire had never happened.

Was that only because of the unpleasantness of the circumstances here at Eton Park?

Or because, beneath that desire, she disliked him still?

Darian breathed out his frustration with the situation. 'Goodnight, Mariah,' he repeated harshly before turning on his heel and leaving the room abruptly, firmly closing the door adjoining their two bedchambers behind him.

Mariah sank back down on to the side of the bed the moment Darian closed the door between their rooms, her thoughts in turmoil. Not because, unpleasant as it was, of the knowledge of those intrusive peepholes in the walls of her bedchamber. Nor was she overly concerned as to what might or might not transpire tomorrow, after the Regent's note of apology had been delivered.

No, the reason for the present disquiet of her emotions was all due to Darian Hunter and the desire she could no longer deny, to herself at least, that she felt for him.

And him alone.

'Would you care to go for a ride, or perhaps a walk, in the fresh air this morning, Mariah?' Darian suggested as he looked across the breakfast table at her.

A breakfast table at which only the two of them sat, the other guests, as Mariah had suggested might be the case, either still asleep after their late night, or choosing to break their fast in the privacy of their bedchambers.

Darian had been awake shortly after seven o'clock, earlier than was usual for him, but as he had expected, he had passed another restless night and, once fully awake, could not bear to stay abed any longer. He had known, from the sounds and soft conversation he could hear in the adjoining room, that Mariah was also awake and talking to her maid.

He had found several peepholes in his own bedchamber the night before and used his handkerchiefs accordingly, but they had both agreed the coverings should come down during the day, if only so that the Nicholses did not realise they both knew of the peepholes.

If the Nicholses' butler—he had introduced himself as Benson, when Mariah had enquired—was surprised to see any of the guests appearing in the breakfast room a little after eight o'clock in the morning, then the blandness of his expression did not show it. He remained as stoically impassive as he had yesterday evening, as he served the Nicholses' guests dinner.

It did not help Darian's peace of mind that Mariah looked beautiful and untroubled this morning, in a russet-coloured silk morning gown, her golden hair swept up and secured at her crown, with clusters of curls at her temple and nape.

She had also been coolly polite to him so far this morning, to the point of irritation.

As if their closeness last night had never happened.

As if Darian had not feasted upon her bared breasts.

As if she had not thoroughly enjoyed having him feast upon her bared breasts.

As if she was annoyed with him for having taken such liberties?

The temper that seemed to burn just below the surface of Darian's emotions whenever it came to Mariah once again raised its ugly head at her lack of response to his suggestion. 'Unless you would rather wait for some of the other guests to come down and perhaps join them?'

Mariah looked at Wolfingham beneath lowered lashes, having sensed that he was angry with her from the moment he knocked briskly on the door adjoining their two bedchambers earlier, then waited for her permission before entering. It had been her experience that Wolfingham did not wait for permission to do anything he pleased.

He looked very severe in his anger. Very much Wolfingham.

The darkness of his hair was brushed back severely from the harshness of his face. His eyes were a flinty, uncompromising green. And there were brackets of displeasure beside his nose and mouth. His movements were also brisk and impatient.

She raised cool brows. 'I shall be quite happy to seek my own entertainment this morning if you are too busy to accompany me on a walk.'

He speared her with that impatient green gaze across the width of the table. 'And what else could there possibly be here to keep me busy this morning?'

Mariah turned to smile at the butler as he lingered by the array of breakfast trays, in readiness for serving them more food. 'Could we possibly have some more coffee, Benson? Thank you.' She waited until the butler had left the room before turning back to Darian. 'If you wish to argue with me, might I suggest that you wait until after we have gone outside,' she hissed in warning.

His brows rose autocratically. 'Why should you imagine I might wish to argue with you?'

Mariah could think of only one reason for

Darian's bad humour this morning: the same sexual frustration she had suffered last night!

She was not completely innocent in the ways of men, knew that a man's passion, once aroused, was apt to make him irritable if it was not assuaged; the housekeeper, Mrs Smith, had once taken a week's leave to visit her sick sister and Martin had been unbearable for the whole time she had been gone. To the point that Mariah had feared he might turn his attentions towards her in the other woman's absence. As a precaution against that possibility, Mariah had wisely taken herself off to the country for the rest of that week.

She could not avoid Darian Hunter's company by doing the same. Not for this weekend, at least.

Nor was she altogether sure she wished to.

She had lain awake in bed for hours after they had parted the night before, her body uncomfortably achy and needy. Her breasts had felt swollen, the tips seeming to tingle and burn, occasionally sending shards of pleasure coursing through her as they rubbed against the material of her night-rail. Between her thighs had felt uncomfortably hot and damp, despite her having used a washcloth before going to bed. And there had been an ache amongst the curls down there that had throbbed even harder when she pressed her thighs together, in an effort to dispel that unaccustomed heat.

For the first time in her life Mariah had suffered what she was sure must be sexual frustration.

And it was both frightening and exhilarating, to realise how attracted she had become to Darian Hunter in such a short space of time. How much she desired him. How much she desired to have him make love to and with her.

That realisation frightened her more than anything else!

She lowered her lashes in case that desire should now be reflected in her eyes. 'I know that you do, Darian,' she answered him quietly. 'And I am sorry for it—' She broke off as he stood up abruptly, his chair scraping back noisily on the polished wooden floor. 'Darian?'

His eyes glittered dangerously as he stood beside the table glowering down at her. 'Exactly

what are you apologising for, Mariah?' he demanded exasperatedly.

She swallowed. 'I realise that last night—that
it did not proceed, as you might have wished it
to have done—'

'As *I* might have wished?' he repeated softly,
dangerously so. 'Are you denying that your own
wishes were exactly the same as my own?'

'I—'

'I advise caution with your answer, Mariah,' he
warned softly, those green eyes glittering dangerously, a nerve pulsing in his clenched jaw. 'I
am not some callow youth who does not *know*
when a woman feels desire.'

Colour warmed Mariah's cheeks and she was
unsure whether it was from embarrassment at
the intimacy of their conversation, or jealousy,
because Darian must have intimate knowledge
of *other* women's desire to be so well informed.
'This is neither the time nor the place for—'

'Will it ever be, Mariah?' he bit out scathingly.
'Will you ever be willing to give yourself to me?'

Mariah drew her breath in sharply even as a
bite of longing twisted almost painfully between

her thighs. What would it be like to give herself to this man? Not just any man, but to Darian Hunter, the Duke of Wolfingham?

Nothing like that horrendous single experience with Martin, she was sure. Even in her limited experience, she knew Darian had already demonstrated that he was a generous and attentive lover, with more of an interest in ensuring his partner's pleasure than taking his own.

Could she give herself to this man? Could she let down her guard, her inhibitions, and open herself up to such intimacy? Such *vulnerability*?

She was starting to believe, that with Darian Hunter, she just might be able to do so…

She straightened her shoulders as she made her decision. 'Perhaps,' she allowed gruffly.

Darian's eyes widened as he barely heard Mariah's softly spoken reply. He had feared the worst minutes ago, as Mariah's eyes once again took on that look of distance, as if she were no longer quite here with him in this room, but somewhere else entirely. Lost in memories, perhaps? Some of them unpleasant ones, if he had read her expression correctly.

Of her husband? Or some other man she had been involved with during her marriage or since?

Darian's ire rose just at the thought of a man, any man, ever having hurt her, in any way.

'Mariah?' He sat down in the chair beside her before taking one of her hands in both of his. Instantly becoming aware of the trembling of her fingers beneath delicate lace gloves—evidence that those thoughts had indeed been unhappy ones? Whatever the reason, he felt heartened by the fact that she did not instantly pull her hand away from his.

'Do you think we could please get out of this oppressive house, if only for a few hours?'

She blinked long lashes. 'I ordered fresh coffee.'

'I am sure that Benson is an understanding fellow. He would have to be to suffer working for the Nicholses!' Darian grimaced.

'Ah, Benson.' The butler appeared in the room almost as if he had been cued to do so. 'The countess and I have decided to go for a walk in the grounds this morning—do you recommend any direction in particular?'

The butler poured fresh coffee into their cups as he answered, his face as expressionless as ever. 'I believe most of her ladyship's guests find Aphrodite's Temple of interest, your Grace.'

'Aphrodite's Temple?' Darian repeated doubtfully; if he remembered his Greek mythology correctly, from his years spent at Eton, Aphrodite had been the goddess of love, beauty and sexuality, but better known as being a goddess who indulged her own selfish sexual desires and lust.

Totally suited to the Nicholses' lifestyle, of course, but not necessarily Darian's own.

'It is Lady Nichols's name for it, your Grace.' Benson seemed to guess some of his thoughts, his expression still stoic and unrevealing. 'It is situated amongst the trees to the left of the lake at the back of the house.'

'Mariah?' Darian turned to prompt, aware that she had not taken part in the conversation as yet. But still Darian felt heartened by the fact that she had allowed her hand to remain in both of his.

She looked up at the butler. 'It sounds…intriguing, Benson.'

She dutifully picked up her cup with her other hand and drank some of the coffee.

The butler nodded. 'And it is always deserted during the day.'

Darian narrowed his eyes. 'But not in the evenings?'

'Not this evening, certainly, your Grace.'

To say Darian was intrigued would be putting it mildly. Although, bearing in mind the sexual games the Nicholses liked to play, he could well imagine that Aphrodite's Temple might prove a little too much for what he now believed to be Mariah's sensibilities. She was much more easily shocked than he might ever have imagined, or hoped for, before spending so much time in her company.

She had become, in fact, the most intriguing woman he had ever met. And was becoming more so rather than less, the more time he spent in her company. It was a certainty he had never been in the least bored when with her.

'Thank you, Benson.' Mariah smiled up at the butler warmly. 'Perhaps you might ask my maid to bring down my pelisse and bonnet from my bedchamber?'

'Of course, my lady.' He bowed.

The silence in the breakfast room seemed charged once the butler had left the two of them alone there. Almost as if the very air itself was waiting expectantly.

For what, Darian was unsure. He only knew that he wanted to get out of this unpleasant and cloyingly decadent household, if only for a few hours. And that he wanted more than anything for Mariah to accompany him.

He stood up, retaining his hold upon her hand as he pulled her up beside him, so close he could almost feel the brush of her hair against his jaw, her perfume once again invading and capturing his senses. 'Ready?'

Mariah's heart leapt in her chest, as she knew instinctively that Darian was asking for more than if she was ready to go for their walk. That he was continuing their previous conversation rather than starting a new one.

Was she ready?

Was she prepared to take their relationship a step further?

To give in to the desires of her own body and engage in intimacy with Darian?

Could she do that?

Or would the memories of the past intrude once again and bring with them the fear and aversion that was all she had known as Martin's wife?

Mariah looked up at him searchingly, not at his handsomeness; that was all too apparent. No, she looked into his eyes, those clear, deep and unwavering green eyes. Eyes that spoke of a man of both honour and truth. A man capable of killing his enemy, if necessary, but totally incapable of physically hurting a woman, most especially one he desired. And Wolfingham did desire her, was making no effort to hide that fact as he steadily met and returned her searching gaze.

Was she ready?

Was it time for her to release her memories of the past, along with her inhibitions, and give in to these new, and at times uncomfortable, yearnings of her own body?

Was she ready to do that?

Chapter Nine

'Good gracious!' Darian winced up at the pale pink marble structure of what could only be described as a miniature copy of the Greek Parthenon he had visited whilst taking the Grand Tour ten years ago or more.

Nestled amongst the woodland to the left of the lake at Eton Park, exactly as Benson had said it would be, it had six small Doric-style marble columns fronting the building, with ten more along each side, and a domed cupola on the roof. And standing in pride of place before the huge wooden doors at its entrance was a nude statue, of what Darian could only assume was Aphrodite, cupping and stroking her own breast.

A nude statue that should not have been there, considering that, if Darian remembered his

Greek mythology correctly, the Parthenon in Greece was dedicated to Athena, the virginal goddess of wisdom and philosophy.

'I can only assume that Lord and Lady Nicholses' knowledge of the Greek gods must be as lacking as their good taste,' Mariah drawled beside him, revealing that her own knowledge on the subject was not lacking at all.

Darian chuckled huskily. 'One does not need to make assumptions once they have seen this.'

Mariah's eyes danced merrily as she glanced up at him. 'It does err rather on the side of ostentatious.'

'That is one word for it!' Darian gave a disgusted shake of his head. 'I sincerely hope that Benson is not of the opinion that the two of us share his employers' bad taste!'

Mariah peered around the statue at the huge oak doors. 'What do you think is inside?'

'Even more lewd statues?'

'Perhaps,' she murmured distractedly as she moved forward to rest one gloved hand on the handle of the door. 'Shall we go inside and see?' she invited huskily.

Darian had to admit to feeling as if a heavy weight had been lifted from his shoulders since leaving the oppression of the Nicholses' household, having enjoyed being out in the fresh air with Mariah walking companionably beside him and wearing a pelisse and bonnet the same russet colour as her gown.

He was in no hurry to forgo that feeling of companionship by entering what he could only assume, in the knowledge of the Nicholses' tastes, and Benson's warning that it would not be empty this evening, was more than likely to be a place where the Nicholses continued their debauchery. 'I doubt it will be any more tasteful inside than out.' He grimaced.

Mariah turned the handle and pushed open the door. 'We will not know— Oh!' She gave a gasp as she stepped inside. 'Oh, do come and look, Darian,' she encouraged breathlessly. 'It is— You will never believe what is in here!'

Darian found himself moving forward to join Mariah inside the temple, partially lured there at having her address him by his first name, something she rarely did voluntarily, but also out of the need to discover exactly what sort of debauchery had awaited her inside and rendered her so breathless.

Darian felt the difference in temperature as soon as he stepped inside—the cavernous marble building was filled with an inexplicable heat. Or perhaps not so inexplicable, as he breathed in the slightly sulphurous smell only thinly disguised by the scent of lavender and realised that the mixture of smells was emanating from the deep sunken bathing pool of water in the centre of the rose marble building.

Mariah's eyes were glowing with pleasure as she turned to look at him. 'I believe it is a natural hot spring!'

That was exactly what it appeared to be. Darian knew that there were a dozen or more of these natural hot springs in England and that society made a point of flocking to them, usually during the summer months, in order to drink or bathe in what they considered to be the health-giving waters.

But he had never before seen or even heard of

there being a private hot spring such as this one obviously was…

He shrugged. 'We are close to Tunbridge Wells, so perhaps this is an offshoot of the one there?'

'It is wonderful!' Mariah drew off one of her gloves before stepping forward to crouch down and dip her fingers into the scented water. 'And it is lovely and warm!' she announced excitedly.

Darian was more than a little grateful for Mariah's distraction with the sunken bathing pool, once his gaze had skimmed over the rest of the interior of the marble building.

There were half a dozen tall candleholders about the cavernous room, fresh candles in them, no doubt in preparation for this evening's entertainments. And a dozen or more slightly raised platforms, each littered with sumptuous and brightly coloured silk cushions.

Darian gave a grimace, his gaze moving swiftly on, as he easily guessed the purpose for *those*.

The two-foot-high frieze on the walls was a plethora of painted scenes of the mythical gods engaged in acts of debauchery with man, woman and beast, as was the domed ceiling above them.

But it was the five statues placed about the side of the pool that now caused him to draw his breath in sharply.

Each and every one of them was of Aphrodite, in all her naked glory, engaged in a variety of sexual acts so explicit that no imagination was necessary and causing Darian's mouth to set grimly.

It was so typical of the Nicholses that they had taken a thing of beauty and turned it into yet another scene for their own very questionable sexual tastes.

'Have you ever seen anything like it before, Darian?' Mariah was totally enthralled by the pool, her expression enrapt, as she moved her bare fingers backwards and forwards in the warmth of the water.

With its dozen or so steps down into the water it reminded Mariah of a painting she had once seen, of Queen Cleopatra bathing in such a pool filled with the ass's milk reputed to have preserved her wondrous beauty.

'No, I cannot say I have ever seen anything quite like this before,' Darian answered coolly.

She turned to look at him quizzically, noting the emerald glitter of his eyes and the slight flush to his cheeks, caused by the warmth of the temple. His mouth was pressed into a thin, uncompromising line. She straightened slowly. 'What is it?'

A nerve pulsed in his tightly clenched jaw. 'We should leave! And continue with our walk,' he added tersely as she looked confused by his vehemence.

Mariah blinked at the harshness of his tone. 'But it is so cosy and warm in here, and surely the perfect place for us to escape the company of the other guests until luncheon.' She had thought Darian had desired to be alone with *her* just a short time ago.

His shoulders were tensed beneath his perfectly tailored dark green superfine. 'I agree that the bathing pool is of interest.'

'But?'

He sighed his impatience. 'But the rest of the temple is far less so.'

Mariah had been so enthralled, so enchanted, at the discovery of the beautiful sunken pool that she had not bothered to look at anything else in the room.

She did so now. And instantly felt the colour heat her own cheeks as she saw the erotic scenes painted on the walls and the ceiling above them. 'I am afraid this has ruined the surprise of the Nicholses' smaller ballroom—' Mariah drew in a sharp breath as she now saw the statues posed about the edge of the pool.

The naked goddess Aphrodite was cradling the head of an equally naked man, whose proportions were worthy of the name Adonis, as he suckled one of her breasts whilst the other hand cupped beneath its twin, thumb and finger in the act of pinching the turgid nipple.

The next was of Aphrodite sprawled upon a couch, the Adonis still at her breasts, her legs parted, a look of ecstasy upon her face as another man feasted on the bounty between her thighs.

Aphrodite reclining upon the same couch, one of the men now lying between her thighs, the hardness of his arousal poised at her entrance— Mariah's gaze moved quickly to the next statue, only to move quickly on again as she saw that

Aphrodite was now posed on her hands and knees, her tongue licking her lips as a man stood behind her holding her hips in place, ready for him to enter her like a stallion covering a mare, whilst another man knelt in front of her, his hard arousal jutting forward—

Mariah ceased breathing altogether, her cheeks burning as her gaze hurriedly shifted to the last statue. She saw that the man behind Aphrodite had now buried himself to the hilt between her thighs, a smile now curving the fullness of her lips as she arched her throat, the huge erection of the second man in her mouth.

'You have never been in here before?' Wolfingham enquired harshly.

'I— No.' Mariah was too stunned still to be able to think straight. Or even attempt the sophisticated response that might have been expected of her! 'No, thank goodness,' she repeated irritably. 'I usually retire earlier than the other guests at these affairs and have never— I have never seen any of this before now.' She waved a dismissive hand, eyes downcast so that she did not have to actually look at those statues again.

Statues that should not have shocked the notorious Lady Mariah Beecham and would surely have amused the sophisticated Countess of Carlisle. And yet Mariah *was* shocked and far from amused.

She was also aware that her thoughts had taken flight as she imagined herself and Darian engaged in those intimacies.

His mouth on her breast.

His mouth feasting between her thighs.

His shaft buried to the hilt between those same thighs.

His entering her from behind with the fierceness of a stallion coupling with a mare.

Mariah's fingers encircling his hardness as she parted her own lips and took that swollen length into her mouth. She turned sharply on her heel, *knowing* her response should have been one of sophistication, and perhaps even boredom, at such an erotic display, but for the moment she was unable to even attempt to be either. 'You are right. We should leave.'

'Mariah?' Darian reached out and grasped her wrist as she would have brushed past him as she hurried to the door.

His gaze was searching on her flushed cheeks, and he drew in a sharp breath as she raised her lashes and he saw the fevered glitter in her eyes. An *aroused* and fevered glitter?

Mariah had presented him with one puzzle after another since the moment they'd first met, it seemed. One moment behaving every inch the sophisticated and notorious woman of society she was reputed to be. The next, as she appeared now, seeming to be as shocked as a girl barely out of the schoolroom, by this evidence of the excesses of the less reputable members of the *ton*.

The more time Darian spent in Mariah's company, the more of a mystery she became to him. And it was a mystery that Darian was fast becoming addicted to solving.

He had no wish for it to be that way. Had no wish to ever become so enthralled by one particular woman that he could think of nothing and no one else.

So enthralled that his every waking thought was of making love to and with her. As the pulsing and throbbing of his erection now testified he wished to do. With Mariah.

Perhaps if he made love with her, witnessed

her in the throes of sexual pleasure, saw that she was a flesh-and-blood woman with carnal needs that matched, or even exceeded, his own, then this hunger would go away?

His fingers tightened about her wrist. 'There is no reason for us to leave here just yet if you wish to remain.'

Mariah's heart leapt in her chest, the heat increasing in her cheeks, as she looked up and saw the burning intensity of Darian's gaze fixed so intently upon her lips. Lips that instantly tingled with the memory of his kisses from the evening before.

Lips that parted instinctively as Darian's gaze held hers captive as his head lowered towards her own.

It was as if the hours between their time together the previous evening and this morning had never happened; the desire was instant. Tongues duelled, hands caressed, their breathing sounding ragged in the silence of the temple as they kissed hungrily.

It was as if they could not get enough of each other. Could not get close enough.

Mariah could *feel* the evidence of Darian's desire pressing hot and heavy against her softness as the kiss continued, tongues tasting, teeth gently biting. She felt the pulse, the thrill, of that arousal, all the way from the top of her head to the tips of her toes. Her breasts swelled, ached painfully, against the bodice of her gown. She felt a gush of wetness between her thighs in response to that desire and she was aware of Darian groaning low in his throat as he now arched, ground that arousal, against and into her.

She felt her folds swell, become wet and slick, as Darian moved one of his hands down and in between them in order to cup her mound through her gown. His palm pressed against her, unerringly finding and putting rhythmic pressure upon the sensitive nubbin nestled amongst her curls, as his fingers curled to trace the delicate folds beneath. Teasing. Caressing.

Mariah wanted more, needed more, as she instinctively thrust up and into those caressing fingers, the pleasure building, growing unbearable as she arched her throat, head back, eyes widening— And instantly found herself looking up at those scenes of debauchery painted upon the ceiling!

It was as if a bucket of cold water had been thrown over her, dousing every measure of arousal and desire as Mariah wrenched her mouth from Darian's to draw in a deep and shaky breath at the same time as she pushed against Darian's chest and put herself at arm's length. 'I do not—' She gave a shake of her head. 'This place makes me feel…uncomfortable.'

Darian's eyes glittered down at her heatedly. 'Uncomfortable or aroused?'

Mariah's breath hitched in her throat and the trembling increased in her limbs. A trembling that Darian could not help but be aware of when his hands were still on her waist. 'A little of both,' she acknowledged gruffly.

She heard Darian draw in his own breath sharply before he answered her huskily, 'I feel the same way.'

Mariah glanced about them at the erotica depicted so graphically on the frieze on the walls and ceiling, and those explicitly erotic statues. And knowing that she could not—

'Not here, Darian. I could not bear to do this here—' She broke off with a shudder. 'I can only imagine the scenes of excess this room has witnessed during the Nicholses' weekend parties! And will no doubt witness again this very night.' She was so tense now that she flinched as one of Darian's hands moved up to cup her cheek before he gently lifted her face up towards his own.

Darian looked down at Mariah searchingly, once again struck by her beauty, at the same time as he recognised those familiar shadows in her eyes and the slight trembling of her lips.

As he also knew that the flush in her cheeks was partly due to the arousal the eroticism in this temple could not help but evoke.

Not completely because of him, or for him.

And it might be a matter of false pride on Darian's part, but when—*if*—he ever made love to Mariah completely, then *he* wished to be the only reason for her arousal.

He drew in a steadying breath before nodding abruptly and releasing her before stepping back. 'Then again I suggest we continue with our walk.'

Mariah was more than a little unsettled by the abruptness of Darian's acceptance of her withdrawal as she led the way out of the marble temple. Could it be that he had actually *wanted* to remain in the temple and indulge in those sexual fantasies depicted by the paintings and statues?

Sexual fantasies that still made the blood boil in her veins and her body ache for—for *Darian*.

Only for Darian.

She had never felt this attraction to any other man. Never felt this ache for a man's touch. Never wanted, hungered for, a physical closeness with any man. Never burned for the promise of pleasure his lips and hands had evoked.

Until Darian.

She looked up at him from beneath lowered lashes once they were outside again in the crisp March air. 'I apologise if my words of earlier led you to expect otherwise, Darian. But I simply could not bear the thought of us being together in such a place.' She gave a shudder of revulsion. 'It was—'

'Unpleasant at best and thoroughly disgusting at worst?' He nodded grimly. 'I thought so, too.'

'You did?'

'I did,' he rasped harshly. 'You may rest assured, I shall be having words with Benson on the subject once we have returned to the house,' he added grimly.

'You are not disappointed?'

A frown appeared between his eyes. 'Why should I be disappointed?'

'I gave the impression earlier—I all but implied—that we, the two of us, might—' She straightened her shoulders. 'I am aware that a man does not take sexual disappointment well.'

'From your husband?'

'No!' Mariah gasped in protest, only to quickly seek composure as she realised how telling her answer might have been. She strived to adopt a derisively dismissive smile. 'No man needs suffer sexual disappointment in regard to his own wife, when the law allows him to do with her whatever, and as often as he wills it.'

Wolfingham's eyes narrowed. 'Were you happy in your marriage, Mariah?'

She eyed him coolly. 'I believe I have already

intimated to you, in a previous conversation, that I was not.'

'Ever?'

Her mouth tightened. 'No.'

Darian could read nothing from the stiffness of Mariah's expression. Or perhaps that stiffness was telling in itself.

'Was Carlisle cruel to you?' He found himself tensing as he waited for her answer.

Her chin rose proudly. 'Only if indifference can be called cruelty. And in the case of my husband, I did not consider it to be so.'

'His indifference? He did not love you?' Darian's gaze sharpened on the paleness of her face.

'No more than I loved him, no.'

'Then why marry him at all?' Darian frowned. 'Your daughter's age now intimates you yourself were barely out of the schoolroom when you married. That it was in all probability your first Season. Surely, as you informed me regarding your daughter, there was no hurry for you to accept the first offer of marriage made to you?' His mouth twisted harshly. 'Or perhaps you fancied yourself as being a countess?'

'No!' Her denial came out sharply this time, her eyes glittering as she looked up at him coldly. 'Sometimes—sometimes we cannot do as we wish but as we must,' she added tautly as Darian continued to look down at her beneath hooded lids.

'And you *must* needs marry Carlisle?'

'*Yes!*' she hissed vehemently.

Darian's gaze narrowed as he studied her intently, looking, searching for the answers he knew Mariah had not yet given him. That the closed expression on her face said she might never give him…

Part of Mariah's mystery was her unwillingness to discuss the past with him. Her past. A past that he was now sure had made her the coolly detached woman she so often was today.

A past that had also led to her being here with him now, acting as an agent for the Crown?

'Talk to me, Mariah. Help me to understand,' he invited gently. 'Explain why you felt you had to marry Carlisle when, as you have said, you did not love him, or he you, and you did not fancy yourself as becoming his countess. Was your family in financial difficulty? Did your father have debts owing to Carlisle directly? Help me to understand, Mariah,' he repeated gruffly.

'Why?'

'Because I *need* to!' he ground out harshly.

'Again, why?'

Darian forced all trace of anger from his voice and expression, already knowing that Mariah did not react well to either. 'Perhaps you might humour me by doing so?'

Her eyes flashed darkly. 'There was nothing in the least humorous about my marriage.'

He sighed. 'Perhaps I chose the wrong word. It would *please* me if you would do me the honour of confiding in me, Mariah,' he amended softly.

She looked at him searchingly for several long seconds, no doubt looking for sarcasm or mockery in his expression, but surely she would find only sincerity.

'Please, Mariah,' Darian encouraged again gently.

She breathed heavily. 'I married Carlisle for none of the reasons you have mentioned.' Her tone was still cold, uncompromising. 'My father was—still is, a very wealthy man. But Carlisle's coffers were bare and he required some of that wealth.' She shrugged. 'Enough to marry a woman he did not love and who did not love him. As might well be expected from such an ill-matched alliance, it was not a happy marriage. For either of us. And that is an end to it.'

Darian doubted that very much. 'And is that the reason you had affairs with other men? Why you now attend licentious weekend parties such as this one?'

'You are being deliberately insulting!' Her cheeks were flushed.

'I am trying to understand.' Darian drew in a deep and controlling breath as he saw the way in which Mariah drew back at his forcefulness. 'Can you not see, I am trying to understand *you*, Mariah,' he spoke more calmly, evenly, knowing his impatience would not endear him to Mariah, or encourage her in the confidences he wanted, needed, to hear from her.

'Why?' She eyed him challengingly. 'What should it matter one way or another whether or not you understand me?'

Darian ground his teeth together. 'It matters to me.'

She smiled without humour. 'That is no answer at all.'

He sighed. 'Can you not see I am puzzled as to why any young and beautiful woman would marry a man she admits she did not love, who did not love her and who was so much older than herself? I could better understand it if Carlisle had been rich and you or your family had been in need. Or even if you fancied yourself as being Carlisle's countess. But you have denied any and all of those as being the reason for entering into a marriage that you admit to knowing would bring you no happiness. I can think of no other reason why—' Darian broke off abruptly, eyes widening as a third alternative began to take form and root in his mind.

A third alternative that would most certainly have required that Mariah *must* marry Carlisle.

Could that possibly be the answer to this puzzle?

Mariah admitted to being four and thirty, and her daughter, Christina, was now aged seventeen, which meant that Mariah could only have been sixteen when that daughter was conceived.

'You were with child when you married Carlisle,' he breathed softly, knowing he had guessed correctly as he saw every last vestige of colour leach from Mariah's already pale cheeks.

Mariah drew her breath sharply, wishing she could deny it, yet at the same time she knew there was no point in her doing so.

Wolfingham had been intelligent enough, determined enough, to accurately guess as to the reason for her marriage to Martin. If she denied it now he would only need to ask any who had been part of society seventeen years ago to discover—to confirm—that the Earl and Countess of Carlisle's daughter had been born not quite seven months after their wedding had taken place.

Her chin rose challengingly. 'Yes, I was with child when Martin and I married.'

Those intelligent green eyes continued to look down at her, searching, probing, as if Wolfingham might pluck the answers to the rest of this mystery from inside her head.

Outwardly Mariah withstood the probe of that astute green gaze, her chin raised in challenge as her turquoise gaze returned his unflinchingly.

But inwardly she was far less secure in her emotions. In being able to withstand these probing questions, coming so soon after they had visited Aphrodite's Temple together. Not just because of those erotic and disturbing paintings and statues, but also because her body was still deeply aroused from Darian's kisses coming so soon after, and the manner in which he had touched her, aroused her, between her thighs.

An arousal, a desire for *more*, that she knew had already battered her shaky defences.

'How was such a thing possible?' Darian breathed softly.

Mariah gave a humourless laugh at the incongruity of the question. 'I believe Christina to have been conceived in the same manner in which all children are!'

Darian reached out to grasp the tops of her arms, relaxing his hold slightly as he instantly became aware of the way in which Mariah was trembling. 'You are avoiding answering the question directly, Mariah.'

Her gaze also avoided meeting his. 'No—'

'Yes,' he insisted gently. 'You did not love Carlisle. Your manner when you speak of him implies that you did not even like him. You have stated that he was indifferent to you and did not love you any more than you loved him. There have been no other children in your marriage. If those were the true circumstances—'

'I do not tell lies, Darian,' Mariah bit out tautly, her chin defensively high, while inside, much as she fought against it, she felt those walls about her emotions slowly but surely crumbling at her feet. 'I abhor it in others and will not allow it in or to myself.'

'Then why, young as you were, would you have given yourself to a man such as Carlisle—' Wolfingham broke off with a gasp, his cheeks taking on a shocking pallor. 'Carlisle took you against your will.' It was a statement, not a question.

It was too much. *Darian* was too much. And Mariah could no longer bear it. She could not look at him any longer!

'No.' Darian's hands tightened on Mariah's arms as she would have pulled away from him, with the obvious intention of escaping. Of possibly returning to the house without him. 'No, Mariah,' he repeated softly, even as he released his grip to instead gather her into his arms as he cradled her close against him. 'We have come so far in this conversation, now we must finish it.'

'Why must we?' She held herself stiffly in his arms.

'Perhaps for your own sake?'

She gave a choked laugh. 'I already know the events of the past, Darian, I certainly do not need to talk of them in order to remember them with sickening clarity.'

'Please, Mariah,' Darian encouraged gruffly, holding back his need to know the truth as he sensed the emotions now raging within her.

He could sense her anger, certainly. Her pain. And perhaps still a little of the desire they had felt for each other earlier? Which, he realised ruefully, was perhaps the only reason that she had not already issued him one of her icy setdowns before marching back to the house. Alone.

Darian's arms tightened about Mariah. 'Was I right when I said that Carlisle took you against your will?'

She drew in a ragged breath. 'Yes.'

'Oh, Mariah,' he breathed out raggedly.

'Carlisle was— I told you, he was in need of funds,' she continued forcefully, as if to ward off any show of compassion from Darian. 'He knew, all of society knew, that my father was extremely wealthy.'

'And?' Darian encouraged gently.

She drew in a ragged breath. 'Can you not leave this alone?'

'No more than I can leave *you* alone,' he assured tautly.

Mariah sighed softly before answering him. 'The Season was only weeks old and Carlisle had danced with me several times at various balls. He could not have failed to know I did not—that I had no particular liking for him. Nor would I ever willingly accept a marriage proposal from him. No matter what his title,' she added ruefully.

Darian was now ashamed of himself for ever

having suggested that might have been her motive for marrying a man so much older than herself. 'It was a natural, if insulting, assumption to have made.'

'Perhaps,' she allowed flatly before continuing. 'Carlisle was not a man to accept a refusal, most especially not from the daughter of a man he, and his family, considered as being so inferior to himself.'

'His family were cruel to you?' If that was so, then it explained Mariah's overprotectiveness towards her daughter's future husband and family.

'They considered me beneath them and treated me accordingly,' Mariah confirmed huskily, licking the dryness of her lips before speaking again. 'Knowing of my aversion, Carlisle lay in wait for me at one of those balls, trapped me alone in a room and—and then he— I will leave you to draw your own conclusion as to what happened next!' She shivered in Darian's arms.

'Mariah?' A black haze had passed in front of Darian's eyes at all that Mariah had not said. That she could not say. 'Why did your father not deal with him? Call him out? Expose him in society for the beast he was?'

'I did not— I dared not tell either of my parents what had happened.'

'Why not?' Darian scowled darkly.

Mariah shook her head. 'My father was very wealthy, but even so he was only a minor landowner, had made his money in trade and was only accepted into the fringes of society, as was I. Carlisle, on the other hand, might not have been rich, but his title made him extremely powerful in society. And if my father had challenged him, or Carlisle had called him out for making his accusations against him, I have absolutely no doubt as to which of them would have walked away.' She gave a shudder.

Nor did Darian; Martin Beecham had been known as an excellent shot and swordsman.

'Besides,' Mariah continued in that same flat voice, 'Carlisle had made it clear to me after— afterwards...' a little colour flared briefly in her cheeks before as quickly fading again '...that if I told my father what had happened, then he would deny my accusations, claim that it was just my own guilty conscience regarding our having acted on our desire for each other. And that the only outcome to my confession would be the one that he wanted anyway, our immediate betrothal and marriage. He also threatened—' She breathed shakily. 'He said he would do *that* again, and again, until I carried his child, so leaving me with no choice but to marry him.'

'The utter and complete bastard!' If Carlisle had been alive today then Darian knew that he would happily have thrust a sword or knife blade through the other man's cruel black heart, for what he had done to Mariah. Or put a bullet in that same warped and twisted heart.

Mariah pressed her face against Darian's chest, causing him to bend lower in order to hear her next words. 'When I discovered just weeks later that I was indeed expecting his child, I wanted to die, to run away. I even thought of ending my own life. And yet I could not do that either, not with the babe inside me. It would have been nothing less than murder. And my father, as Carlisle had predicted, once told of my condition could not refuse the earl's offer of marriage. Not without causing scandal and ruin for all of us. I was well and truly trapped. Into marrying a man I not only hated, but also had every reason to fear—' She broke off as a sob caught at the back of her throat.

Darian inwardly cursed himself for having forced the subject to the point that he had put Mariah through the pain of reliving those unhappy memories of her past.

The memory of the taking of what Darian was sure would have to have been her young and inexperienced body.

A body that now trembled almost uncontrollably against his own as Mariah battled to stop the tears from falling.

Darian had no doubt they were tears Mariah should have shed eighteen years ago. For the manner in which she had lost her innocence. For the babe, conceived in fear on Mariah's part and greed on Carlisle's.

For the twelve years of unhappiness she had spent as wife to the very man who had raped her.

Chapter Ten

Darian shifted slightly so that his arms were beneath Mariah's thighs and shoulders as he lifted her up and against his chest before striding across to sit down on one of the ledges along the outside of the temple. He settled Mariah comfortably on his thighs, her head, for the moment, resting against his shoulder.

Darian held on to her tightly. 'I believe it would be better if you now tell me all, Mariah, when you have already come so far.'

She gave a shake of her head. 'And I do not care to talk, or think, any more about those horrible memories.'

'The memories of when Carlisle raped you. What he did was the rape of an innocent, Mariah, nothing more, nothing less,' Darian insisted grimly as she stiffened in his arms.

'I am well aware of what it was.'

'After which, he then forced you into years of suffering an unhappy marriage with him, because of your daughter.' Darian could barely contain the violence he felt at learning of Carlisle's brutish behaviour. An impotent violence, in view of the fact that Carlisle was no longer alive to feel the lash of his tongue or the flash of his blade. Carlisle might have been an excellent swordsman, but Darian knew he was better.

'I may not have wanted the marriage, or Carlisle, but I have loved Christina since the day she was born,' Mariah instantly defended. 'She has always been the one shining light in my life.'

Darian nodded, only too well aware of the protectiveness she felt towards her daughter.

As he was also now aware of her reason for objecting so vehemently to the idea of Lady Christina marrying anyone at the age of only seventeen years. The same age as Mariah had been when she was forced to marry Carlisle.

'But there was no heir?' Darian prompted slowly.

'Carlisle did not— He had no interest in my producing his heir. He had a younger cousin he was perfectly happy should inherit the title. His only reason for marrying me was to attain a portion of my father's considerable fortune.'

'I have noted that marriage has a way of producing children, whether they are wanted or not,' Darian drawled ruefully.

'And I have already told you that Carlisle was completely indifferent to me as his wife.'

Darian looked down at Mariah with incredulous eyes. 'Are you saying— You cannot possibly mean—'

'What, Darian?' Mariah lifted her head to look up at him, her eyes dark and shadowed in the pallor of her face. 'I cannot possibly mean that my husband's uninterest in me was such that he did not share my bed, even once, after we were married?' Her smile was completely lacking in humour as she gave a shake of her head. 'Why can I not mean that, Darian, when it is the truth?'

A truth that Darian could not even begin to

comprehend, when his own desire for Mariah was such that he found it difficult to sleep at night, to stop thinking about her day and night, of the ways in which he wished to make love with her. She had been Carlisle's *wife* for twelve years. Surely the other man could not have—

Mariah took advantage of his distraction to pull herself abruptly out of his arms before standing up and turning the paleness of her face away in profile, a shutter seeming to have come down over her emotions—no doubt because she deeply regretted having revealed them in the first place.

'Why should Carlisle have need of the attentions of his very young and very inexperienced wife,' she continued drily, 'when his mistress of over twenty years was the housekeeper of our London home?'

'Carlisle kept his mistress in your home after you were married?' Darian stood up slowly.

It was well known that many gentlemen of the *ton* kept a mistress after they were married. But never, ever, in the same house as their wife. It was not done. It simply was not done. And yet, it appeared that that was exactly what Carlisle had done.

'In truth, I was grateful for Mrs Smith's existence.' Mariah shrugged dismissively as she briskly pulled her glove back on to the hand she had earlier dipped into the heated pool. 'And I was not made uncomfortable by the arrangement, visiting London rarely during the first ten years of our marriage. I much preferred to remain in the country with Christina.'

Darian breathed deeply. 'But something happened to change that? Did you and Carlisle perhaps reconcile?'

'There was nothing *to* reconcile.' She turned to frown at him. 'How could there be, when we had never been husband and wife in the true sense of the word?'

'But something did change.'

Mariah knew she had said too much already, revealed too much—more than she had ever told anyone else about the past and the reason for her marriage to Martin. The only thing she had not shared with Darian was Martin's treasonous behaviour. And the lie that was the rumour of her numerous affairs…

She had never confided as much to anyone about the past as she now had to Darian Hunter. Knew she had only been lulled into doing so this time because her emotions had already been disturbed by what she had seen and done in the temple. From her imaginings as to what it would be like to engage in those acts with Darian. Imaginings that had deepened, flourished, during the kiss that had followed.

And that momentary weakness had now cost her dearly.

Damn it, she had told him of Carlisle's brutality. Her forced marriage. She had *cried* in Wolfingham's arms. She, who never cried, preferring never to show any sign of weakness. To anyone.

And she did not intend to continue to do so now where Wolfingham was concerned, either. Had made a vow to herself long ago not to allow *anyone*, apart from Christina, to come so close to her, to know her so well, they were capable of hurting her. 'Do you still wish to continue with our walk, or has all this ridiculous emotion

dampened not only your shirt but your enthusiasm for walking?' she prompted coolly.

That astute green gaze remained narrowed on
her as Wolfingham stepped closer. 'There was
nothing in the least ridiculous about your upset
just now, Mariah.'

'And I believe it to have been an utterly ridiculous waste of time,' she insisted coldly, 'when
the past, talking about it, changes nothing.'

'And what of the future, Mariah?' He stepped
so close to her now that she could feel the warmth
of his breath against her brow. 'What of *your* future?'

She gave a dismissive shrug. 'Once this weekend is over, I do not believe that to be any of your
business.' Mariah clasped her hands together so
that Darian could not see they were trembling
still, evidence that her emotions were not as back
under her control as she would have wished them
to be. Her complete lack of control, just minutes
ago, now made her feel vulnerable, in a way she
found most disturbing.

Wolfingham raised his hands to cup both her
cheeks before he tilted her face up so that he

might look directly into her eyes. 'And what if I wish to make it my business?'

Wolfingham's gentleness was unbearable, before and again now, when Mariah knew her emotions, despite her denials to the contrary, remained ragged and torn. When her *defence* against Darian's gentleness remained ragged and torn.

'I am sure I am not the first woman to have been trapped into an unhappy marriage,' she said drily. 'Nor will I be the last. And as you say, I did become a countess because of it.'

'Do not attempt to make light of it, Mariah!' Wolfingham rasped harshly.

'How do you wish me to behave, Darian?' Her eyes flashed darkly as she looked up at him defiantly. 'I have wailed and railed, and now I wish to forget it. As I have forgotten it these past seventeen years.'

'Did you forget, Mariah?' He looked down at her searchingly. 'Did you ever really forget what that man did to you?'

Of course Mariah had never forgotten. She had

not wanted to forget, was the woman she was today because of it.

Her chin rose. 'Enough so that I do not require, or need, your own or anyone's pity because of it.'

'Does this feel like pity to you?' Wolfingham had grasped one of her hands and placed it over the noticeable bulge in his pantaloons. 'Does it?' He pushed for an answer, his eyes glittering down at her darkly.

'And how long will that desire last, Wolfingham?' Mariah fell back on derision as her defence as she deliberately removed her hand at the same time as she returned his gaze mockingly. 'Until you have sated your lust between my thighs and then wish to move on to some other conquest? Possibly to a woman who is younger and less complicated!'

He gave a slow shake of his head. 'I find your complications intriguing and your age of four and thirty is unimportant to me.' A nerve pulsed in the tightness of his jaw. 'And I resent your assumption that my desire for you is a fleeting thing.'

'Perhaps I presume as much because it has

been my experience that a man will say anything, promise anything, when he wishes to bed a certain woman.' She eyed him scornfully.

Darian frowned his frustration. He did not give a damn what Mariah's previous lovers had told her, or promised her, when *he* was the man now standing before her, telling her, physically *showing* her, how much he desired her. How much he desired to *be* with her.

A desire of such intensity that Darian had no doubt it would not abate for some time. If ever.

More than anything he wished to take Mariah to his bed. To gently kiss her, caress her, to *taste* her, to worship every satiny inch of her, and show her the depth of his desire for her. And then he wished to start all over again. And again. And then again. Again, and again, and again, until Mariah was left in absolutely no doubt as to the depth of his desire for her.

At the same time as he knew that this place, Eton Park, with its peepholes into the bedchambers and a temple worthy of the debauchery of the Roman Empire at the height of its power, and the guests to match, plus the Nicholses' intrigues, was not where he wished to lie with Mariah the first time. Not where he wished to make love with her, to worship her and her body, as she so deserved to be worshipped.

His hands fell back to his sides as he stepped back. 'Very well, we will continue with our walk for now. But we will talk on this subject again once we are back in London,' he added softly.

She arched a taunting brow. 'Not if I do not wish to do so.'

Darian's mouth quirked into an equally mocking smile. 'A word of advice, Mariah. I am not like any of your previous lovers. When you know me better, which you most assuredly will, I believe you will find that I am a man who *always* means what he says as well as *always* keeps his promises!'

Mariah masked her uneasiness as she fell into step beside him as he began to walk back in the direction of the lake, very much afraid that Darian Hunter was indeed a man who always meant what he said as well as kept all of his promises.

Afraid?

Oh, yes, Mariah was very much afraid, in spite

of everything that had happened between them since they first met, that she desired Darian Hunter as much as he now claimed to desire her.

That she desired to know Darian in a way she had never desired any other man.

'Do try to smile, Darian, rather than scowl and glower in that dark and disapproving way,' Mariah advised lightly later that afternoon, viewing his reflection in the mirror after he had entered her bedchamber through the door adjoining their two rooms, after only the briefest of knocks. His appearance was elegantly foreboding in a black superfine, grey waistcoat and pantaloons. 'Else, once we arrive downstairs for tea, the other guests will think that the two of us have argued.' She looked at her own reflection in the mirror to give her already perfectly styled hair another pat, rather than continue to look at Darian's more disturbing reflection.

Everything about this man disturbed her.

The way he looked.

Her undeniable response to his touch.

The desire she was finding it more and more difficult to deny or control.

And the fact that she had confided so much of her past to him earlier today.

That breach in the barrier she had kept so firmly about her emotions for so many years disturbed Mariah most of all, so much so that she had spent the past four hours, since they parted downstairs after returning from their walk, attempting to shore up or replace that barrier.

Only to have taken but a single glance at Darian's reflection in the mirror as he strode forcefully into her bedchamber just now to know that those efforts, determined as they might have been, had been a complete waste of her time.

What was it about this man in particular that affected her so? Oh, he was handsome enough. Forceful enough. But he was far from the first handsome or forceful man to have expressed a desire to bed her. Desire she had found absolutely no difficulty in rejecting in the past.

No doubt because she had not felt a return of that desire for any of those other men.

The same desire that had so shaken and disturbed her earlier, to a degree that she had confided more of her past to this man than she had ever wished anyone to know.

The very same desire that made her feel so vulnerable whenever she was in his presence.

'I have absolutely no interest in what they do or do not think,' Darian answered her impatiently now, the scowl still dark upon his brow as he stepped further into the room.

Mariah turned slowly, a slight frown creasing her own brow now. 'Has something happened?'

Darian stared at her incredulously.

Had something happened?

As far as Darian's life was concerned, Mariah Beecham had happened.

So much so that just one look at her, when he entered her bedchamber just seconds ago and saw how beautiful she looked in an afternoon gown of the palest turquoise, her breasts a creamy and tempting swell, the very low and curved neckline of that gown revealing the tops of her nipples as being a deep rose, and he was forced to endure a hard and painful throb inside his pantaloons yet again.

At the same time he felt a ridiculous desire to cover up those beautiful breasts, so that no other man could look at or see any part of them. Or become aroused and tempted by looking at them, as he undoubtedly was.

A ridiculous reaction, when Mariah's coolness towards him this morning, once they had left the temple, and then completed their walk about the lake together in complete silence, had spoken only too clearly not only of her need to put a physical distance between them, but also of a return of that emotional one.

Darian had lingered in the hallway to have that promised word with Benson while Mariah went up the stairs alone. By the time he arrived up the stairs, the door to Mariah's bedchamber, and the door adjoining their two rooms, had both been firmly closed. He had known instinctively that Mariah meant them as a barrier between the two of them. One he crossed at his peril.

Because she had revealed too much about herself to him this morning? Because he now knew things about her life, her marriage to Carlisle, that perhaps no one else did?

Darian did not believe that Mariah was the type of woman who would confide her deepest, darkest secrets easily. To anyone. And he knew from personal experience that Mariah's role as an agent for the Crown would also make it difficult for her to have close friends, male or female, for fear they might discover her secret.

The murderous rage Darian had felt earlier today, towards Martin Beecham, had not abated in the slightest in the hours that had passed since Darian and Mariah had parted so stiffly. Her husband had been an out-and-out bastard who had raped and terrified a young and inexperienced girl for the sole purpose of forcing his child and marriage on her, trampling all of the young girl's romantic dreams into the dust beneath his own greedy need for the bride's portion of her father's money.

Not only that, but Carlisle had doubly insulted Mariah by having his mistress in residence as housekeeper in one of the homes Mariah herself had necessarily to visit on occasion.

How did any woman survive that? But especially one as young and innocent as Mariah had been then?

Darian knew it would be difficult for a woman of any age to have survived such base and selfish cruelty.

Yet here Mariah stood before him, a lady in every sense of the word. So graciously beautiful, as well as being the most desirable woman he had ever known.

Nor was it any wonder, after all that she had suffered at Beecham's hands, that Mariah had turned to the comforting arms and desire of other men, both during and after her marriage.

Had any of those other men *made love* to her? Darian wondered as he continued to admire her beauty and poise. Truly made love to her? Showering Mariah with the gentleness, the care and consideration that was her due?

Or had they all without fail, as she had so scathingly scorned earlier, treated her as just another conquest in their bed? So that they might afterwards claim, to their male friends and associates, to have bedded the beautiful Countess of Carlisle?

'Darian?' Mariah prompted again, her expression having become wary at his continued silence.

Darian had spent most of the past four hours pacing his bedchamber and thinking of Mariah. Of all that she had told him of her past, at the same time as he now knew it was that past that had made her the woman she was today: cool, poised and determined to remain totally removed from emotional entanglements with any man.

It had brought Darian to the question that concerned him the most: how the two of them were to now proceed—or *if* Mariah would allow them to proceed at all.

For he had promised himself he would not use any type of force upon Mariah. That he might perhaps allow himself to cajole, tease and seduce her, but he would not, could not, ever use coercion or force of any kind.

'Nothing has happened.' He drew in a ragged breath. 'I want— I need— No, I *ask*—' He broke off abruptly, only now appreciating how difficult it was going to be to keep the promise he had made to himself earlier, when just to look at

Mariah again made his blood burn in his veins and his erection throb.

Mariah was now truly alarmed by Darian's behaviour. Of what might possibly have happened to put the arrogantly assured Duke of Wolfingham in such an obvious state of uncertainty. 'Yes?' she prompted tensely.

He straightened his shoulders, emerald gaze fixed intently upon her as he spoke abruptly. 'I would ask if you will allow me to kiss you before we go downstairs?'

Darian Hunter was a man Mariah had every reason to know was always and completely assured as to the rightness of his own actions.

As he had believed he was in the right two weeks ago, when he had warned her not to encourage his younger brother in his attentions to her.

As he had believed her friendship with Aubrey Maystone must be one based on intimacy.

As he believed her to be a woman who had indulged in many affairs, both during and after her marriage.

Wolfingham had believed he was in the right in all of those things.

Admittedly, he had already been proven wrong in two of those things, but the latter? Darian still believed in that legion of lovers Mariah was reputed to have had these past seven years, no doubt believed them to have been her comfort for the coldness of her marriage.

And yet he now asked if he might kiss her?

To say Mariah was flustered by Darian's request would be putting it mildly. Especially when she had every reason to know that the arrogantly self-assured Duke of Wolfingham never 'asked' permission to do anything, let alone asked permission to kiss *her.* The notorious and scandalous Mariah Beecham, Countess of Carlisle…

She attempted a sophisticated and dismissive laugh, hoping Wolfingham did not recognise it, as she certainly did, as sounding more nervous than assured. 'I thought we had agreed not to continue with that conversation until after we have returned to London.' She gave a pointed glance to where her shawls and handkerchiefs were once again draped over those peepholes into her bedchamber, in order to preserve her privacy, both while she'd bathed and changed her clothes earlier.

A nerve pulsed in his tightly clenched jaw. 'I find that my desire to at least touch you again cannot wait that long.'

His desire to touch her again!

It was Wolfingham's touch that had been her undoing from the beginning. Not just once, but so many times. On the terrace of her own home. In the guest bedchamber of her home, where he had necessarily to stay in order to recover after his collapse. In the gallery of Lady Stockton's home. And here. Here at Eton Park she had allowed Darian to touch her more intimately than any other man had ever done before.

Mariah now feared her response to his touch.

Not because she thought Darian would ever physically hurt her—she was already sure he would never use force upon any woman. She had come to know him these past two weeks, knew he was not a man who showed his strength or power through physical dominance over others, but by the sheer force of his indomitable will.

No, she did not fear Darian would physically hurt her, as Carlisle had hurt and humiliated her, to such an extent she had never cared to repeat the experience.

Darian Hunter was capable of hurting her in a much different way.

She was not only aroused by him, felt desire for him, she also liked and admired him. His strength. His honesty. His family loyalty. His devotion to his country. He was, as she had learnt these past weeks, in all things an honourable man.

A man she might love.

And Mariah did not wish to love any man, even one as handsome and honourable as she now knew Darian Hunter, the Duke of Wolfingham, to be.

The independence of nature she so enjoyed now had been hard won, after years of living only half a life, hidden away in the country, and for the most part ignored by the husband she hated and despised. For the past seven years, since revealing Martin's treasonous behaviour to Aubrey Maystone, she had no longer had reason to fear Martin, or anything he might try to do to her. Aubrey Maystone had taken care of that.

For the first time in her life Mariah had done exactly as she pleased, her worthwhile work for the Crown enabling her to become a woman she could not only respect, but also like.

For her to fall in love, with any man, would, she believed, be to put all of that at risk.

To fall in love with Darian Hunter, the much respected and admired Duke of Wolfingham, would most certainly lead to heartbreak on the day he cast her aside and left her for another female who had caught his fancy.

Wolfingham might have a reputation in society as being severe and very proper, nor had there ever been any gossip as to his ever having taken a permanent mistress. But that did not mean there had not been other rumours, of his liaisons with several ladies of the *ton*, and the gaming hells and the houses of the *demi-monde* he had visited on the evenings he spent with the other Dangerous Dukes.

Dangerous.

Yes, where Mariah was concerned Darian

Hunter more than lived up to his reputation as being dangerous. To her independence. To her untutored body. To her untouched heart.

And that she could not, dare not, allow.

'Goodness, Wolfingham, where on earth has all this politeness and solicitude come from?' she taunted him mockingly. 'If it is because of our conversation earlier today, then let me assure you that it is of no consequence.'

'No consequence?'

'Absolutely none,' she dismissed coolly in the face of his vehemence. 'It was too many years ago to be of any significance to the here and now. Nor, as I assured you earlier, do I have need of anyone's pity. Least of all your own,' she added with deliberate scorn.

'Least of all mine?' Wolfingham's eyes were steely now as he looked at her through narrowed lids.

'But of course.' Mariah returned that hard gaze with a challenging one of her own. 'You really are arrogance personified if you believed otherwise. In the circumstances I described to you earlier, a woman can either grow stronger from the experience or allow herself to be beaten down by it. I am certain that by now you know me well enough to have realised which one of those women I have become?' She arched haughty brows.

Oh, yes, Darian knew full well which one of those women best described Mariah. Her fortitude was only one of the reasons he admired and liked her so much. Desired her so much. A desire she was now at pains to inform him she wanted no part of.

To a degree she would not even give permission for him to so much as kiss or touch her again.

Was that avoidance not telling in itself?

Or was he simply grasping at straws, because he so much wished for Mariah to return his desire?

It was a question Darian intended to explore with all thoroughness once they were well away from Eton Park.

He nodded. 'As it is almost five o'clock, might I suggest that we join the other guests downstairs for tea?'

A surprised blink of Mariah's long dark lashes was her only outward sign that she was surprised at his ease in accepting her refusal. 'But of course.' She nodded graciously as she collected up her fan before sweeping past him and preceding him out of the bedchamber.

Darian smiled grimly as he followed her out into the hallway before offering her his arm to escort her down the stairs.

Mariah might believe him to have been routed by her set-down, but if she had come to know him half as well as he now knew her, then she would very soon realise that his patience, in achieving his goals, was infinite.

And his most pressing goal, desire, was to make love with Mariah.

Chapter Eleven

'If one knows where to look, it is almost possible to see the bruises in the shape of fingerprints upon Lord Nichols's neck,' Mariah remarked conversationally a short time later before taking a sip of tea from her cup, as she and Wolfingham sat together on a *chaise* in the Nicholses' salon. Its placement by one of the windows allowed them to observe the other guests.

'He's lucky he still has a neck to bruise,' Wolfingham muttered, the ice in his gaze the only sign of his displeasure, as he gave every outward appearance of relaxation, lounging on the *chaise* beside her.

Mariah chuckled softly. 'I am not sure I ever thanked you properly for your gallantry last night.'

He turned to face her. 'No, I do not believe you did,' he drawled drily.

'Well, I do thank you.' Mariah was unnerved to once again find herself the focus of those piercing green eyes. 'These people really are an unpleasant lot, aren't they?' Her gaze now swept contemptuously over the other guests.

The men were drinking brandy instead of tea, with most of them already well on their way to being inebriated yet again. Including their host, as he occasionally cast a furtively nervous glance in Wolfingham's direction.

The women were once again wearing an assortment of gowns that would be more suited to a bordello or brothel. Not that Mariah had ever been in either establishment, but she could well imagine the state of *déshabillé* of the women who did.

Normally Mariah would have had no difficulty in maintaining a certain distance, from both the gentlemen's drinking and the ladies' state of undress, when attending one of these weekend parties. She had no doubt it was the challenge her coolness represented to the gentlemen that caused the *ton*'s hostesses to continue to include her in these weekend invitations. The gentlemen made no secret that they began each of these weekends with a wager on which one of them might succeed in bedding the Countess of Carlisle.

Yes, normally Mariah would not have the slightest difficulty maintaining that distance.

Wolfingham's presence, and Mariah's complete awareness of the lean and muscled length of his body as he lounged on the *chaise* beside her, had heightened her senses to such a degree, she now seemed to feel and view everything as if through a magnifying glass.

The way in which even the statuary and decor in this house seemed to be attuned to the debauchery that went on under its roof.

The gentlemen's red and bloated faces, and their avidly glittering eyes as they ogled the ladies' state of undress.

Those same ladies vying with each other, with more and more outrageous behaviour, in order to attract and hold the attention of the gentleman, or gentlemen, they had decided to bed.

The way in which Wolfingham's austere handsomeness, in the formal black of his clothing and snowy white linen, succeeded in putting him above any and all of the other gentlemen present.

Knowing that, *aware* of that, this weekend, and Mariah's forced association with Wolfingham, could not come to an end soon enough for her.

'Very,' Wolfingham now drawled disdainfully. 'I feel soiled just by being in the same room with them.'

Mariah arched a mocking brow. 'And yet you and the other Dangerous Dukes are rumoured to frequent brothels and the houses of the *demimonde*.'

His eyes narrowed. 'I draw the line at brothels. And the ladies of the *demi-monde* do not pretend to be upstanding members of society.'

Mariah's curiosity was piqued by the fact that he had not denied frequenting *those* houses. 'Do you—'

'And what are you two whispering about together so secretly?'

Without either of them having been aware of it—Darian was sure that Mariah's attention had

been as focused on him as his was on her—
their hostess had crossed the room to join them
and now stood looking down at them with coquettish curiosity. A lapse in concentration on
their part, which Darian knew could have been
very costly indeed, if they had chanced to be
talking of their real reason for being here this
weekend.

He stood up politely and instantly regretted
doing so as his superior height gave him a clear
view down the front of Clara Nichols's loose
gown, as far as her navel—decidedly *not* an
arousing sight. 'We were discussing the…mer-
its of the temple in your garden, madam.'

Lady Nichols's rouged lips gave a knowing
smile. 'So *that's* where the two of you have been
all day.'

'This morning, at least.' Darian gave an acknowledging nod. 'Your butler was most help-
ful, this morning, in telling us of its existence.'

'Benson *has* turned out to be a treasure.' His
hostess smiled fondly at the butler as he circu-
lated amongst the guests, calmly refilling the
gentlemen's brandy glasses with the same aplomb

as he did the ladies' teacups, before withdrawing from the room with that same calm after one of the footmen had entered and drawn him aside to speak to him quietly. 'One is never quite sure, when one takes on new household staff, whether or not they are going to suit, but Benson did come personally recommended and he has more than lived up to it these past few months.' Lady Nichols turned to eye them speculatively. 'I trust you both enjoyed our little temple?'

'Most diverting,' Darian answered noncommittally, a glance at the clock on the mantelpiece revealing that it was just a few minutes after five o'clock, time for the Prince Regent's note to be delivered, for which he and Mariah had been patiently waiting these past twenty-four hours. And, hopefully, the reason Benson had been summoned from the room?

Well, the waiting had perhaps not been quite so patient, on Darian's part! Indeed, it had been unimaginable torture, having to suffer the company of such people and made all the worse by his increasing desire for Mariah. His only wish now was to have this charade over as soon as was possible, so that they might return to town and he could concentrate his considerable attention on seducing Mariah.

'You will have the opportunity to return there later on tonight, of course,' Lady Nichols continued to chatter. 'It is *so* romantic in the evenings.'

Darian almost choked on the sip of brandy he had been about to take, at the very idea of the erotica displayed in that temple ever being thought of as romantic. Certainly it appeared that Lady Nichols's idea of romance, and his own, differed greatly!

How long did it take Benson to collect the Prince's note of apology from the rider and return with it?

'We are both so looking forward to the masked ball this evening, Clara.' Mariah claimed their hostess's attention as Darian made no reply.

'And I trust that you will not remain quite so… exclusive…this evening, sir?' Lady Nichols gave Darian's arm a playful tap with her fan. 'There are many more ladies present who would welcome your attentions.'

Darian narrowed his gaze on her. 'Indeed.'

Where the hell was Benson with the Prince's note?

'Oh, yes.' Their hostess gave another of those tittering giggles, so incongruous in a woman who was aged in her forties, at the least. 'Indeed, the ladies have talked and speculated of nothing else since your arrival yesterday.'

'Indeed?' Darian repeated stiltedly, his hands clenching tensely into fists at his sides.

'Oh, my goodness, yes!' Lady Nichols looked up at him with what she no doubt thought was a winning smile, obviously having absolutely no idea how close Darian was to telling her to go to the devil and take her simpering flirtation with her! 'I myself would dearly love to—'

'I do believe Benson is trying to attract your attention, Clara,' Mariah put in hastily, having thankfully spotted the butler approaching them, a silver tray held aloft on one hand; the increasing coldness of Darian's expression, and those hands clenched at his sides, warned Mariah he was seriously in danger of telling Clara Nichols exactly how repugnant he found both her and her guests. Their reason for being here be damned!

'What *is* it, Benson?' Their hostess could barely contain her irritation at the interruption as she frowned at her butler.

'This was just delivered for you, madam.' Benson offered the silver tray. 'I took the liberty of asking the rider to wait, in case there is a reply,' he added helpfully.

Mariah could feel Darian's tension as the two of them watched their hostess break the seal on the letter before quickly scanning its contents. Mariah actually held her breath as she waited for Clara Nichols's response, which for the moment appeared to be only a displeased frown.

'What is it, my dear?' Richard Nichols called out across the room.

A pout appeared on Clara Nichols's too-red lips. 'The Prince Regent is unable to attend the ball this evening, after all. Some urgent business requiring he return to town earlier than expected.'

There were several murmurs of 'too bad' and 'bad show' from the other guests, but it was

Richard and Clara Nichols whom Mariah continued to study intently, as she knew that Darian did also.

'That is a pity.' Richard Nichols strolled over to join his wife before reading the note for himself. 'Oh well, can't be helped, old girl.' He patted his wife awkwardly on the shoulder. 'The country's needs must come first and all that.'

Lady Nichols continued to pout her disappointment. 'It really is too bad of him,' she snapped waspishly. 'I only invited Lady Henley on his instructions I should do so.'

'I am sure that there are plenty of other gentlemen present to keep that lady entertained. Hey, Wolfingham?' Richard Nichols attempted a conspiratorial and conciliatory smile at the haughty duke.

'You are welcome to do so, by all means, Nichols.' That smile was not returned as Darian looked coldly down the length of his nose at the older man. 'As I am sure I have made perfectly clear, I am happy in the company of Lady Beecham.'

'A man can have too much of a good thing,

though, don't you think?' Nichols suggested slyly.

Wolfingham's jaw was tight. 'No, I most certainly do not think,' he bit out tautly, eyes glacial as he continued to look contemptuously at the other man.

A contempt, a danger, that Mariah knew the older man would be foolish to ignore. Most especially so when he still bore the bruises on his neck from the last time he had managed to infuriate Wolfingham.

She stood up to tuck her gloved hand into the crook of Darian's arm, administering a gentle squeeze of caution even as she turned to smile at Richard Nichols. 'I am afraid our…friendship… is relatively new, Lord Nichols, and Wolfingham is quite besotted still.' She felt the tension in Darian's arm beneath her fingertips as his response to such a ridiculous claim.

As it was indeed ridiculous to think of the haughty Duke of Wolfingham as ever being besotted with any woman, least of all the scandalous Countess of Carlisle!

'Well, can't blame a man for that.' Richard

Nichols wisely backed down. 'Oh, do cheer up, Clara,' he turned to instruct his sulking wife impatiently. 'I am sure we shall manage quite well this evening without the Prince's presence. After all, we do have the elusive Duke of Wolfingham as one of our guests!'

'So he is.' Clara Nichols brightened before turning to the waiting butler. 'There is no reply, Benson.' She placed the note back on the tray. 'Could you see that this is put in my private parlour?' she added dismissively.

'Of course, milady.' The butler bowed politely before withdrawing.

Mariah frowned her puzzlement as she continued to study Richard and Clara Nichols; there did not seem to be any undue reaction to the Prince's note of apology, apart from Clara's obvious disappointment.

Clara Nichols now directed another of those coquettish smiles at Wolfingham. 'Where were we?'

'I believe that Mariah and I were about to return upstairs,' he bit out tautly.

'Again? So soon?' Clara Nichols gave Mariah

an envious smile. 'My, he is a lusty one, isn't he, my dear?'

Mariah felt the warmth of colour enter her cheeks and dearly hoped that the other woman would see it as the burn of anticipation at being the recipient of Wolfingham's passion, rather than the embarrassment it really was. 'I am sure we are both very grateful to you for allowing us the privacy, in which to fully indulge ourselves, this weekend.' She curled her nails painfully, and quite deliberately, into Darian's tensed arm.

He moved his other hand to cover hers, squeezing with just enough pressure not to cause pain, but to administer a warning of his own. 'Very grateful,' he drawled drily.

'We appear to be completely superfluous here, my dear. Shall we return to the entertainment of our other guests?' Richard Nichols extended an arm politely to his wife. 'If you will both excuse us?' He bowed politely to Mariah and Wolfingham as the other couple moved away, Clara Nichols still twittering her disappointment over the Prince Regent as they did so.

Mariah waited only long enough for the Nicholses to be out of earshot before turning to Darian. 'Should we not wait here awhile longer before returning upstairs?'

'No.'

'But—'

'I believe we have seen all that we needed to see, Mariah,' he assured grimly.

'We have?'

He nodded tersely. 'Besides which, if I do not leave this company very soon, then I am afraid I might lose my temper completely.'

Mariah could see the truth of that claim in the dangerous glitter of his eyes and the nerve pulsing erratically in his tightly clenched jaw.

She held her head high as she accompanied him across the room, knowing they were being observed with interest as she heard the outbreak of whispering and laughter in the room behind them as they stepped out into the hallway. 'Must you always be so—so *obvious* as to our supposed intention of disappearing to make love together?' she hissed the moment they were out in the deserted entrance hall.

Darian was feeling murderous rather than

obvious. How much longer must he endure this torture, of watching men like Nichols lusting after the woman he—the woman he—the woman he what? Exactly what was it that he felt towards Mariah?

Protective, certainly.

Proprietary.

Possessive.

To the extent he could quite cheerfully have taken on every man in that room who had so much as looked at Mariah sideways—which was all of them, damn it!

'You are missing the point, Mariah.'

'And it *appears* to me that you are enjoying yourself altogether too much at my expense!' she came back heatedly.

'Could we talk of this further once we reach your bedchamber?' he prompted softly as Benson appeared at the top of the stairs, no doubt after having delivered Lady Nichols's letter to her private parlour.

'May I get you anything, your Grace?' he offered politely as he reached the bottom of the staircase.

'No, thank you, Benson,' Darian answered distractedly, his hand firmly beneath Mariah's elbow as he pulled her up the stairs beside him.

'Darian?'

'You are missing the point, Mariah,' he repeated through gritted teeth as they reached the top of the staircase before turning into the hallway leading to their adjoining bedchambers.

'Which is?' she prompted as she opened the door to her room.

'The letter,' he reminded impatiently as he followed Mariah into her bedchamber. 'The response to the Prince's letter.' He closed the door firmly behind him.

All of Mariah's indignation fled as she realised she had indeed allowed her embarrassment to distract her, that she was the one now guilty— however briefly!—of forgetting their reason for being at Eton Park at all this weekend. 'Apart from Clara's obvious disappointment as hostess that the Prince would not be gracing her ball tonight after all, there did not appear to be any response at all to his note,' she stated belatedly. 'No pointed looks, or conversation, with anyone else in the room. No one hastily leaving the room. There was no response whatsoever.'

'Exactly.' Wolfingham paced the room restlessly.

Mariah continued to frown. 'Does that mean Aubrey Maystone's information was wrong?'

'Maystone is never wrong,' he assured grimly.

'Then what happened just now?'

'Nothing. That is the problem.' Wolfingham looked grim.

Mariah chewed briefly on her bottom lip. 'Do you think that might be because someone suspects that we—'

'Came back upstairs to make love?' Wolfingham interrupted huskily. 'Oh, I think that was more than obvious, my love.'

Mariah blinked, momentarily confused at the sudden change in his tone. 'What—'

'I am sure that we have been more than obvious in our obsession to bed each other,' Wolfingham acknowledged indulgently. 'Indeed, I find I cannot wait another minute to undress you and make love with you,' he added gruffly, at the same time as the fierceness of his gaze

now moved pointedly to the shawls and handkerchiefs Mariah had left in place over the peepholes about the bedchamber. 'Come over here,
love,' he invited huskily.

A warning to Mariah that someone was standing behind one of the walls at this very minute,
listening to their conversation?

And necessitating in their continuing with the
act of lovers once again eager to be alone together, so that they could make love?

Oh, heavens!

She gave an abrupt nod of her head, in silent
acknowledgement of their eavesdropper, as she
crossed the room to Wolfingham's side. Her heart
was pounding loudly in her chest, her pulse rac-
ing, as she wondered for how long, and how far,
they would need to continue with their act of
eager lovers.

At the same time she felt an inner yearning to
satisfy, just a little, the desire she had discovered
she felt for Darian.

All thoughts of anything else fled Darian's
head as Mariah now stood in front of him, so
close he could feel her breath brushing warmly

against his throat as she moved up on tiptoe. 'Oh, yes, Mariah,' he groaned in approval—both of her quickness of mind, in realising they were not completely alone, *and* most certainly of the fact that her teeth were now nibbling in earnest on the sensitivity of his earlobe; surely an unnecessary embellishment to their act when they could be overheard, but not observed?

He turned his head slightly so that he could look into Mariah's eyes, the fullness of her parted lips now just inches beneath his own as their gazes clashed and held, both of them breathing softly, expectantly.

Darian took full advantage of Mariah's closeness as his arms moved about her waist to pull her in tightly against him, his gaze continuing to hold hers as his head lowered and he took fierce possession of those parted lips with his own.

Something Darian had wanted—*hungered for*—since they had parted so coolly after their walk earlier today.

So much so that there was no way to stop the avalanche of desire that now swept over and through him as he felt Mariah's lips part beneath his own, her arms about his waist.

Darian deepened the kiss, his tongue sweeping, tasting her parted lips, before plunging, thrusting into the moist heat beyond.

Mariah tasted of the honey cake she had eaten with her tea; sweet and utterly delicious. Combined with her exotic perfume, it was addictive.

Darian continued the depth of those kisses as, for the second time that day, he swept her up into his arms. Carrying Mariah across the room before placing her on top of the bedcovers and following her down. Settling his thighs between her parted ones, he took his weight on his elbows before cupping either side of her face with his hands and continuing to kiss her hungrily. Tasting, sipping, possessing!

Mariah gave a throaty groan as Darian's lips and tongue continued to claim her own. Even as his hands deftly removed the pins from her hair before loosening it on to the pillows beneath her, she moved her arms up over his shoulders as her fingers became entangled in the dark silkiness of his own hair.

She was filled with a yearning ache as the heat of Darian's arousal throbbed between her parted thighs. Pressing, shifting slowly against and into her, pleasure surging through her as that friction stroked against the throbbing nubbin between her now slick and swollen folds.

Darian broke the kiss, breathing heavily as moist lips now travelled the length of her throat. 'God, how I want you!' he groaned achingly. 'You are so beautiful, Mariah. So very beautiful.' One of his hands now moved caressingly, restlessly, beneath the curve of her breast, before pulling down that silken barrier to bare their fullness, his hand now cupping her breast in sacrifice to his questing lips and tongue.

'Darian!' Mariah's back arched off the bed as he claimed one aroused and sensitive nipple into the heat of his mouth, pleasure surging, filling her, as his tongue flicked against that hardened nub, teeth gently biting before he suckled deeply, drawing the whole of her nipple into the heat of his mouth.

Darian's mouth was heat and fire, pleasure beyond description. A pleasure that surged and intensified unbearably between Mariah's parted thighs, causing her to arch up against his hardness, in need of a greater friction as she searched, ached for the full promise of that pleasure.

'Yes!' she cried out as Darian shifted slightly to her side, his lips and tongue still drawing fiercely on her breast as his hand moved to push her gown up her thighs. Caressing, seeking, *finding* the opening in her drawers that allowed his fingers access to caress the slick moisture of her swollen folds, at the same time as the soft pad of his thumb stroked the throbbing nubbin above. 'Please, Darian! Yes!' Mariah was mindless with pleasure as she arched up into those caresses, wanting, needing, something *more*.

'Come for me, Mariah,' Darian encouraged throatily at the same time as first one finger, then two, entered the slickness of her core. 'Please come for me, Mariah!' He suckled hard on her nipple at the same time as those fingers now moved rhythmically, his thumb stroking, pressing down on that swollen nubbin above.

Pleasure, unlike anything Mariah had ever known, or imagined, now exploded between her thighs, her head thrashing from side to side on the pillows as that release coursed hotly, claiming the rest of her body in wave after wave of seemingly endless pleasure.

She was still lost to the wonder, the euphoria of that pleasure, as Darian gazed down at her darkly before sliding down the length of her body until he knelt between her parted thighs. Mariah offered no resistance as he slowly pushed her gown up to her waist before moving aside to allow for the removal of her drawers and bared her to his heated gaze as he parted her legs so that he might once again kneel between them.

'So pretty. Like a rose in bloom,' he murmured appreciatively as his fingers moved to part her swollen folds, allowing him to gaze his fill of her before he lay down between her thighs, his tongue a hot and pleasurable rasp against her highly sensitised and aroused flesh.

'Darian?' Mariah felt she should protest at such intimacy, but in truth she felt so satiated still, so lost in wonder as she felt the stirring of her arousal for a second time in as many minutes, that she could barely speak, let alone offer words of protest.

'Let me.' The coolness of his breath was sweet torture against her hot and aching flesh. 'You are so beautiful here, Mariah,' he groaned as he touched her gently. 'So beautiful!'

His lips and tongue caressed her at the same time as his hands moved up to cup her breasts. Mariah gazed down in wonder as those long fingers and thumbs tweaked and pinched her swollen nipples, at the same time as Darian's head was buried between her thighs, the sight of such intimacy enough to cause her to gasp anew.

'Again, Mariah,' he encouraged roughly. 'I want you to come for me again.'

Mariah felt captured, swept along in a relentless tide as a second wave of pleasure built higher deep inside her and then higher still. Higher and higher—

'Darian!' Her back arched to push her breasts into Darian's hands, encouraging, welcoming the pleasure-pain as he now squeezed and pinched her nipples to the same rhythm as her thighs moved into the stroking of his lips and tongue.

She gave a gasp, eyes wide with shock as plea-sure even more intense than the first suddenly ripped through her.

This was what all the poets wrote about so ar-dently. What singers crooned about so achingly. What lovers so hungered for they were willing to throw away all caution and reputation in order to achieve it.

Mariah had never known, never guessed, that lovemaking, this wonderful feeling of comple-tion, would be so all-consuming. So much so that nothing else mattered, the outside world, and ev-eryone in it, ceasing to exist. Only Darian and Mariah remained at that moment.

'Oh, goodness.' She groaned weakly as she remembered that the two of them were not *all* that existed in the world, that they had a listen-ing audience.

Darian raised his head to look at her, his face flushed, lips moist and slightly swollen from ministering to Mariah's pleasure. 'He or she left some time ago,' he assured gruffly, pulling her gown slightly down over her legs before he moved up the bed to lie down beside her.

Mariah looked at him anxiously. 'How do you know?'

'I heard the click of the door shutting as they left. I did not spend all my afternoon in my bedchamber, but explored those peepholes and passages' he explained as her eyes widened. 'I would never allow anyone to see or hear your pleasure but me, Mariah,' he assured softly as he lifted a hand to smooth back the hair at her temple.

Mariah felt grateful for Darian's reassurances, even as she trembled at the full realisation of what had just happened between the two of them. What she had all but begged to happen, as she arched and thrust against the caress of Darian's mouth and hands.

She should feel mortification just thinking of those intimacies. Should feel embarrassment, if not horror, at her own wanton response and encouragement of those intimacies. Her complete lack of inhibition.

Mariah could feel none of those things.

Instead, for the first time in her life, Mariah felt totally fulfilled as a desirable woman. A desired and now totally satiated woman.

It was exhilarating.

Liberating, in a way Mariah had never imagined.

So much so that there was no room inside her for embarrassment or self-consciousness.

Darian Hunter, the austere and exacting Duke of Wolfingham, had just made thorough love to her. Had touched and caressed her more intimately than any other man had ever done. Than any other man had ever wanted to do. And he had not found her wanting.

Wolfingham had not found her wanting.

For so many years Mariah had wondered if it was because she was so undesirable that Martin had never wanted a normal marriage with her. Not that she had ever wanted a normal marriage with the man she had considered as being her rapist, but Martin's complete lack of interest in her physically, and for so many years, had certainly caused her to question her own desirability.

Oh, she had played her part well these past seven years, had flirted and teased whichever gentlemen had needed to be flirted with and teased, in order for her to extract the information from them that she needed. But she had never felt like this with any of those other men, never *wanted* as she had wanted with Darian. Never felt even tempted with those other men, had known that she would just be another conquest to them.

In contrast, Darian had made love to her like a thirsty man in a desert, praising her all the while, telling her time and time again how beautiful she was to him. How much he desired her. How much he wanted and appreciated her body.

Gifting Mariah with that freedom, that liberation in her own sexuality that she had long believed dead inside her.

And in doing so Darian had given her pleasure unlike anything Mariah had ever known before.

A pleasure she now fully intended to gift back to him.

A seductive smile curved her lips as she recalled that look of bliss on the male statue's face as Aphrodite took his full and burgeoning length into her mouth.

Chapter Twelve

Darian did not believe he had ever seen anything as beautiful as Mariah looked at this moment; her loosened hair was a golden halo about her flushed face, her eyes soft and languid, her cheeks creamy smooth, her lips slightly swollen from their earlier kisses, her breasts still bared to the heat of his gaze. Perfectly rounded and pert breasts, tipped with ruby berries still puckered and reddened from his ministrations.

And beneath all that visual beauty was the smell of her pleasure and that tantalising and erotic perfume that Darian associated only with her.

The hardness of his shaft shifted, surged, as he continued to breathe in that perfume and gaze down at those perfect and desirable globes, as a painful reminder that his own arousal still needed to be dealt with. And sooner rather than later.

'You are very sure our eavesdropper has left?' Mariah murmured as she obviously felt that impatient movement of his arousal against her thigh. She sat up beside him to gaze down at that telling bulge in his pantaloons, her breasts still fully exposed to Darian's heated gaze, resulting in another fierce pulsing of his aching arousal.

Darian had been fully aware of Mariah's initial resistance to give in to the pleasure he offered, when she believed they had a listening audience. 'Very sure,' he confirmed gruffly.

'Then I believe it is now my turn to pleasure you.' Her fingers moved to unfasten the buttons of his pantaloons, the bared fullness of her breasts jiggling tantalisingly at the movement. 'I would not wish for anyone but me to see or hear your own pleasure, either...' she added softly.

'Mariah?' Darian placed one of his hands over both of hers as he looked up at her searchingly, wondering if she really meant what he thought she did.

He had bedded his first woman at the age of sixteen and there had been too many more women since then for him to remember all their faces, let alone their names. Several ladies of the *demi-monde* had also chosen to take him into their mouth and give him pleasure that way. Could Mariah really be suggesting she might do the same?

Just the idea of having Mariah placing those delectable and pouting lips about his shaft, of having her suck him into her mouth and all the way to the back of her throat, excited Darian to such a pitch he could barely contain it.

Mariah could see that she had momentarily surprised Darian with her intentions. Because, despite the licentiousness she had witnessed during this, and other weekend parties, most of the ladies of the *ton* were believed to be too delicate, too prim and proper, to be exposed to such acts as she had witnessed earlier today between those statues in Aphrodite's Temple?

Mariah's newly found pleasure and sexual liberation, her curiosity, was now such that she *must* know all. Whether or not she would be any good at this was another matter, but she fully intended to make up with enthusiasm what she lacked in experience.

Mariah looked down searchingly into Darian's face, noting the glitter to those dark green eyes as he looked back at her, the flush to his cheeks.

And knowing that her own eyes were probably just as fevered, her cheeks as flushed. In anticipation of freeing, of seeing, that enormous bulge inside Darian's pantaloons...

She had never seen that part of a man in the flesh, so to speak.

She had not seen Darian naked as yet, but even so a glance down at that telling bulge in his pantaloons told her he was so much bigger than Martin had been.

'Do not think of it, Mariah,' Darian rasped abruptly, his hand gentle on her cheek as he turned her averted face back towards him. 'The past has no place here between the two of us, Mariah,' he assured softly.

Mariah continued to look at him blankly for several long seconds, held captive by those memories, those awful, painful, disturbing memories.

'You shall be in charge here and now between the two of us, Mariah,' Darian assured her huskily. 'Or not. It is your choice to make. I assure you no one shall make you do anything you do not wish to do,' he promised gruffly as his hands dropped down to his sides. 'I am yours to do with exactly as you wish, Mariah. Or not,' he repeated gruffly.

'But—you have not found your own pleasure yet.' She frowned. 'Once aroused, I believed men to need that release more than a woman?'

Darian had to once again fight down his murderous feelings towards Martin Beecham. Because Mariah required his gentleness now, rather than a show of the anger he felt towards her dead husband. For having inflicted, over so many years of his indifference, such an uncertainty of her own sexuality, her desirability. A cruelty indeed to such a beautiful and courageous lady as he now knew Mariah to be.

Darian sat up slightly to run the soft pad of his thumb over the fullness of her bottom lip to take any sting from his next words. 'You do not have to do anything else, Mariah. I can return to my bedchamber and deal with my arousal myself,' he assured gently.

Her eyes widened. 'You are talking of— You would—'

'Yes.' He smiled at her reassuringly.

'You have done that before?'

'Many times. All young boys do it,' he dismissed without embarrassment as her eyes widened. 'Indeed, I believe it becomes their favourite pastime during adolescence.'

'But it has been many years since you were that age.'

Darian shrugged. 'A man's member tends to wake up before him each morning. And without a wife to ease that arousal, it often becomes necessary for a man to take himself in hand.'

'I see,' she said slowly. 'And which would you prefer now, to feel your own hand or mine?'

Darian drew his breath in sharply at the candour of her question. 'Neither. I would prefer to have your mouth on me, Mariah,' he explained as she looked at him questioningly.

Delicate colour bloomed in her cheeks. 'As would I.'

Darian groaned low in his throat as he watched Mariah moisten her lips, as if in anticipation of the act. 'May I watch? It would enhance my own pleasure to do so, Mariah,' he explained as she gave him another of those curious glances.

Curious and slightly shy glances, which to Darian's mind did not sit well with the reputation of her being the scandalous and adulterous Countess of Carlisle.

The gossip of Mariah's adultery Darian could now understand, when her husband had been such an out-and-out and indifferent bastard to the needs of his own wife. That curiosity and shyness needed explaining—

All thoughts fled Darian's mind as Mariah moved up on her knees beside him so that she might place several pillows behind his head, her bared breasts jutting forward pertly as she moved, allowing her nipples to dangle, so swollen and tempting, just inches away from his rapidly moistening mouth.

'Give me just a taste of you first, Mariah!' he groaned achingly.

Mariah tilted her head as she looked down at

Darian, easily noting that his fevered gaze was now transfixed on her bared breasts. She leant forward slightly in order to allow one of her nipples to touch his moist and parted lips, gasping slightly as he instantly suckled that fullness into his mouth, eyes closing, lashes resting darkly against his flushed cheeks, as his hand cupped beneath that breast as he drew hungrily on the nipple.

And allowing Mariah to learn another sexual revelation…

That a man could be just as vulnerable during lovemaking as a woman.

Perhaps more so, she realised, as she turned her head so that she might guide one of her hands to untie the ribbon on Darian's drawers, before turning back the folds of those drawers and finally exposing that impressive bulge.

Darian's shaft was incredibly long and thick as it jutted up from its nest of dark curls.

Mariah licked her lips. What would he taste like? Salty or sweet? And would—

'Darian!' She gave a sudden gasp as she felt a now familiar burn of pleasure growing, swelling, between her own thighs, Darian's mouth almost painful on her nipple as he suckled deeply, hungrily, teeth biting as his other hand alternately stroked and then squeezed its twin. 'Darian, I believe I am going to—'

'Come for me, Mariah!' he urged fiercely, both hands cupping her breasts now, squeezing and pinching her nipples as he gazed up into her flushed face.

'I—' She cried out her pleasure as another climax suddenly ripped through her body, the longest and strongest yet, as her empty sheath contracted and pulsed hungrily, again and again, the swollen nubbin above throbbing. 'I had no idea I could— That it could happen so—so spontaneously.' She rested her head weakly on Darian's shoulder.

It had never happened for Darian with any other woman before now. But as he now knew only too well, Mariah was indeed a woman unlike any other. And the fact that he had been able to give her such pleasure, just by touching her breasts, gave him more satisfaction than he could describe.

Not that he had time to dwell too long on those feelings of wonderment as Mariah now moved sinuously down the length of his body, her bared breasts briefly resting either side of his fiercely jutting erection before she moved to lie between his parted thighs and take him in hand.

'You are so wondrously big,' she murmured admiringly as she stroked the length of him. 'Your skin so velvety soft,' she added huskily before wrapping the fingers of both hands about the thickness of his engorged and throbbing length. 'And so wet.' The soft pad of her thumbs stroked over the tip of his shaft.

Darian felt his groin tighten as her fingers continued to caress him sensually. 'Mariah!' he groaned harshly, tensing, as he watched her little pink tongue flick out to taste the tip.

'Would you like me to stop?' Her glance up at him, from beneath her long lashes, was wickedly teasing.

'No!' Darian protested, groaning as he saw her smile widen, his head falling back on the pillows as he watched her continue to lick him, her tongue a sensuous rasp across his highly sensitised skin, her long golden hair cascading forward to drape sensuously across his thighs.

'You taste delicious,' she murmured appreciatively, her breath hot against his dampness.

'As do you,' he assured gruffly.

'Really? Let me see!' She moved quickly up the bed to lick her own juices from his parted lips. 'Mmm.' She nodded, her smile sensuous as she moved back down the bed to kneel between his thighs, before once again taking him in hand and holding him up as she parted her lips and took him into her mouth, her lips tight just beneath the tip and stretched tautly about his thickness.

Darian groaned, hips bucking, the second he was engulfed by the heat of Mariah's mouth, totally unable to stop himself from thrusting up rhythmically into that wet heat. His hands clenched into the bedclothes at his sides as he fought to hold off, to prolong the moment of his release.

An almost impossible task as he watched Mariah's head bob up and then down. Up and then down. Each time taking him deeper and then deeper still, her tongue swirling, dipping, as she rose up, before plunging him deeper on the downward stroke. Little by tortuous little, until he finally hit the back of her throat and she began to suck in earnest.

Finally, when Darian thought he might go insane from the pleasure, she released him on the next upward stroke, eyes dark as she looked up at him at the same time as she moved one of her hands lower, caressing him tenderly. 'Come for me now, Darian,' she invited as her gaze held his at the same time as she parted her lips and slowly took him to the back of her throat.

Darian felt the tingling at the base of his spine, the painful tightening through his groin, and knew his climax was imminent. 'You must release me now, Mariah—'

Her own second and throaty 'Now!' vibrated down the length of him, sending Darian spiralling over the edge, totally unable to stop from coming as he became lost in the fiercest, most prolonged orgasm he had ever experienced in his life.

Mariah continued to suck on him greedily,

cheeks hollowed, and she refused to release him until she had swallowed down all of Darian's salty-sweet release. Even then she could not resist licking the last few drops from the tip before sitting back on her heels to look up at him.

His dark hair was dishevelled, the dark curls lying damply tousled on his brow. Eyes glittered the colour of emeralds between sleepy half-closed lids, his cheeks were flushed, his lips parted. His body was completely relaxed and exposed to her as his erection lay half-hard still against the tautness of his stomach.

He was beautiful.

Completely satiated, wickedly decadent and utterly beautiful.

And she had done this. She, Mariah Elizabeth Beecham, Countess of Carlisle, had given Darian Hunter, the severe and oh-so-proper Duke of Wolfingham, that look of satiation.

A thrill of satisfaction rose up beneath Mariah's breasts, filling her chest to bursting, in the knowledge that she had succeeded in giving Darian the same pleasure he had given her.

'Come up here and lie beside me, Mariah, and

let us both catch our breath,' he invited gruffly now as he opened his arms to her.

Mariah moved up the bed gladly before lying down at his side, her head resting on one broad shoulder, one of her arms draped across the muscled hardness of his stomach as he stroked the long tendrils of her hair. She had never felt so relaxed, never known such peace as this existed, as she glowed in the aftermath of their lovemaking.

This, this closeness, was what it should be like between a man and a woman. What she had been denied for so many years.

What she had denied *herself* for so many years, too afraid to risk this vulnerability with any man. A vulnerability that Mariah now knew applied to both the man and the woman; a man could not be any more vulnerable than when he allowed a woman to take that precious part of himself into her mouth and pleasure him. As she had been just as vulnerable when she'd allowed Darian to pleasure her in the same way.

Such intimacies required complete trust, from both the man and the woman.

As Mariah had learnt to trust Darian.

Not just with her body, but with the secrets of her past, as well as her work for the Crown. She had not told him all of her secrets, of course. Had not, for instance, confided that Martin had been a traitor to his country. Or revealed that that awful time with Martin had been her only physical experience with any man before today. But she had trusted Darian with so much more than that.

Had told him what had happened to her the night of Christina's conception.

Trusted him with the knowledge Aubrey Maystone had imparted, of the work she had carried out secretly for the Crown these past seven years.

Mariah believed she could trust Darian never to reveal those secrets to another living soul.

As she now trusted him with her life.

With her love?

Mariah tensed, barely breathing, as she considered what her feelings were for the man beside her. For Darian Hunter, the severe and sober Duke of Wolfingham.

She did trust him, yes. She also admired him.

Truly believed he was a man she could trust with her life.

But with her love?

No!

Mariah dared not allow herself to fall in love with any man. It was too much of a vulnerability. Too much power—

'Mariah?' Darian could feel her sudden tension as she lay so still beside him. 'What are you thinking about?' he prompted gently.

She made no answer for several long seconds before replying huskily, 'Do you think the person listening to us behind the wall might have been the assassin?'

'In all probability, yes,' he bit out grimly. 'Damn it, I shall have to send a note to Winterton Manor informing Aubrey Maystone of these most recent events.'

They both knew that the reason he had not already done so was because they had been too engrossed in each other, in the desire between them.

'I shall do so as soon as I have regained the strength to get out of bed and go down to the stables in search of my groom,' Darian added.

'Is it possible, as we were followed up the stairs, that perhaps we have not been as clever in our deception of being lovers as we had hoped to be?'

Darian did not believe for a moment any of this conversation had been the reason behind Mariah's sudden tension a few minutes ago; she had paused too long, considered her words for too long, before answering him. Nor was he insensitive to the fact that she seemed to be distancing herself from him once again, despite still being held in his arms, her half-naked body draped alongside his own, her hand resting warmly— trustingly?—on his chest.

At the same time he was aware of how tenuous still was the closeness between the two of them, despite the depths of the intimacies they had just shared. That unless he wished to call Mariah a liar and risk alienating her even further, he had no choice but to accept this as her explanation for her sudden quiet.

For now…

'From the speed with which they left, once the two of us began to make love, I believe they

can have no further doubt regarding the latter—
Mariah?' he questioned again sharply as he felt
her increase in tension. He turned on his side
to look at her searchingly, easily noting the pallor of her cheeks, the shadows in those beautiful turquoise eyes, before she lowered her long,
dark silky lashes and hid those shadows from
his view. 'Do you regret what just happened between the two of us?'

She moistened her lips with the tip of her
tongue—tasting him there, as Darian could still
taste her on his own lips? The colour that suddenly warmed her cheeks, as she became aware
of her movements, would seem to imply that she
did.

'I accept it was necessary,' she answered him
evenly now. 'If we were to successfully keep up
this pretence that we are lovers.'

'It is no longer a pretence, Mariah!' Darian
felt stung into snapping his frustration with her
coolness. With the fact that they both knew there
had been no need for the continuation of that pretence, once he had assured Mariah their eavesdropper had departed.

She swallowed, those long lashes still hiding the expression in her eyes. 'We have shared... certain intimacies. That does not make us lovers.'

'Then what does?' Darian scowled down at her darkly. 'I will admit that this was far from the ideal place, or situation, for the two of us to have become lovers,' he continued impatiently, very aware that he had previously decided he could not allow such a thing to happen at Eton Park. But he could no more have resisted, denied himself the pleasure of making love to and with Mariah just now, than King Canute had been able to turn back the tide! 'But that does not change the fact that it is now exactly what the two of us are,' he added huskily.

Mariah drew in a ragged breath even as she gave a definitive shake of her head. 'I believe we have allowed the licentiousness and erotica at this place to colour our judgement. That once we return to town we shall both see how...ridiculous such a relationship would be between us.'

'Ridiculous?' Darian knew the frown had deepened on his brow.

'Of course.' She gave a dismissive laugh as

she finally looked up at him, those eyes reflecting her derision. 'We have absolutely nothing in common outside of this current situation. No common interests, or friends. Indeed, in London you are every inch the austere and sober Duke of Wolfingham as I am the scandalous Countess of Carlisle.'

Having come to know Mariah better, Darian was now extremely sceptical about the latter.

'And this?' He reached out to grasp the tops of her arms. 'What was it that just happened between the two of us?'

'A very enjoyable but unrepeatable interlude,' she dismissed drily. 'As I have said, I believe we have both allowed our forced alliance, along with the licentiousness of our surroundings, and the people here, to arouse and cloud our better judgement. Left to our own devices in town, the two of us would never have so much as spared each other an approving glance.'

Darian could not deny that his opinion of Mariah, before meeting her, had been far from favourable. Nor had that opinion changed once he *had* met and spoken to her, despite the unwanted and begrudging desire he had felt for her.

But sometime during these past few weeks his opinion of Mariah *had* changed. Dramatically. He now knew her to be a woman of great courage and fortitude. A woman who risked her own life and reputation, on a daily basis, in order to work secretly for the Crown. For that alone Darian might have admired and respected her.

But there was so much more to Mariah than that.

Darian now knew that she had also fought her own personal demons of the past and not just survived them, but had become a gracious lady of great dignity and personal independence.

Much like a soldier after a success in battle.

Truly, Darian believed Mariah to have as much courage, to be as heroic, as he or any of his four closest friends had been in their fight against tyranny, openly and secretly.

None of which changed the fact that Mariah was now rejecting, out of hand, the very idea of the two of them continuing any sort of relationship once they had returned to town.

A rejection, the challenge of her expression, as she met his gaze so fearlessly, he would do well to heed.

Darian had never been one to back down from any sort of fight. Least of all one that mattered to him as much as this one did. As much as continuing to see Mariah, to be with Mariah, now did.

But she was absolutely correct in one regard. This was not the time, or the place, for them to have this conversation. There was too much else at stake: a would-be assassin in this house they still had to identify and bring to justice.

As such, Darian would agree to delay the conversation between himself and Mariah.

For now.

Once they had left Eton Park and returned to town, he had every intention of pursuing a satisfactory conclusion to this conversation.

Of pursuing Mariah.

Chapter Thirteen

'Does our hostess seem less than composed to you this evening?' Darian murmured softly to Mariah, eyes narrowed as he observed a rather red-faced Clara Nichols across the crowded ballroom, as she issued low-voiced instructions to a somewhat panicked-looking young footman.

A small ballroom that, along with the hundred or so masked and indecently clothed guests laughing and talking too loudly, was every bit as outrageously decadent as Mariah had earlier warned him it would be.

The walls were all mirrors, reflecting back the dozens of candles illuminating the room, as well as the lurid and explicit frescoes painted on the ceiling above. Although to Darian's way of thinking, it was hard to decide which was worse, those erotic frescoes above, or the half-clothed guests milling about below.

He had certainly breathed a sigh of relief once he had realised that Mariah's gown, a delicate gold confection of some gossamer material to match the gold of her mask, was actually not as revealing as it at first appeared.

Her beautiful and creamy shoulders were completely bare, admittedly, but there was at least a bodice to the gown, albeit a sheer and delicate lace that did little to hide the fullness of her breasts and rouged nipples below. But the body of the gown was at least lined, with only the barest hint—literally!—of the silky limbs and blonde curls hidden beneath.

With things so unsettled between the two of them still, Darian did not believe he would have been able to hold on to his temper if he also had to cope with other gentlemen ogling Mariah's near nakedness!

'She does,' Mariah now answered him equally as softly. 'Perhaps I should stroll over and see what is amiss?'

Darian's first instinct was to say no, to keep

Mariah safely beside him, rather than risk her moving through the crowded room, and the possible groping hands of the other gentlemen present, to where their hostess stood beside the doorway.

There was also a would-be assassin still somewhere in their midst.

Darian quickly repressed his overprotectiveness, knowing that Mariah would no more accept that than she had wished to listen to his conversation earlier, in regard to the continuation of their relationship once they were back in town. He had no doubt that she would especially baulk at any sign of possessiveness towards her on his part. Even if that was exactly how he felt!

Just the thought of any other man but himself so much as looking at Mariah with more than admiration was enough to cause his jaw to tighten and his back teeth to grind together.

'We shall both go,' he compromised as he held out his arm to her.

Mariah eyed Darian from behind her mask as she placed her gloved hand on his arm before allowing him to escort her across the crowded ballroom, knowing that the avidly covetous eyes of at least a dozen other women followed his progress.

He was, without a doubt, the most handsome and striking-looking gentleman in the room, formidably so.

Once again dressed all in black, accompanied by snowy white linen, the mask that covered the top half of Wolfingham's face was also a plain and unrelenting black, green eyes glinting warningly through the two eye-slits to ward off the approach of any of the other guests.

Mariah repressed a shiver at just how devilish Darian looked this evening. Dark and watchful. Cold and unrelenting.

Nothing at all like the warm and satiated man who had made love to her, and to whom she had made love, earlier this evening.

'Cold?' Darian turned to her solicitously as he obviously felt her shiver.

Mariah straightened determinedly; after all, she was the one who had insisted there was nothing between them but the intimacy of the circumstances under which they now found themselves.

She was a little disappointed, hurt, at how easily Darian had accepted her dismissal after making only a token protest, but that was for her to deal with, not him. Darian had promised nothing and she had asked for nothing, which was how it should be. How it *must* be, if she was to continue to maintain her emotional independence.

'Not at all.' She now gave him an over-bright smile. 'Did you manage to send your groom with a note to Winterton Manor?' she prompted softly.

'Yes,' Wolfingham confirmed. 'Although he has not returned as yet with Maystone's reply,' he added grimly.

'Do you think that something might have happened to him along the way?' Mariah frowned; Aubrey had told them that Winterton Manor, where the older man had waited these past twenty-four hours or so, along with several other of his agents, until he heard word from them, was only situated five miles or so from Eton Park.

Darian frowned. 'We shall go out to the stables and check for news of his return, once we have talked to Clara Nichols.'

Mariah's brows rose. 'Surely there is no reason for both of us to go?'

Perhaps not, but Darian still felt that reluctance to leave Mariah's side. 'We shall both go, Mariah,' he repeated uncompromisingly, returning the searching glance Mariah gave him with one of cool determination.

Darian sensed an underlying air of tension in the Nicholses' ballroom this evening, one that smacked almost of desperation. As if someone in this room knew they were being hunted. And if anything amiss was about to happen, then Darian intended being at Mariah's side when and wherever it did.

'Very well.' Mariah finally nodded acquiescence, her eyes narrowing as they approached their flustered hostess and her obviously nervously trembling footman.

'Something definitely has Clara on the verge of a fit of the vapours,' she murmured softly to Darian, her voice rising as they reached Clara Nichols's side. 'Clara, darling, whatever is the matter?' She left Darian's side to link her arm companionably through the older woman's.

Lady Nichols dismissed the footman before answering. 'Oh, Mariah,' she wailed. 'Nothing this evening is going as it should, and— Oh! Good evening, your Grace,' she greeted hastily as she saw Darian was standing just behind Mariah.

'Can the countess and I be of any help?' he queried lightly, senses now on full alert, knowing it was most unusual for ladies of the *ton* to become so discomposed in front of their guests, no matter what the situation.

'Oh, no!' Clara Nichols looked horrified at the suggestion. 'No, thank you, Wolfingham,' she added with more calm. 'It was just a— There were several domestic matters in need of my attention. It is all settled now.'

Mariah somehow doubted that, from the hunted look still in Clara Nichols's pale and constantly shifting blue eyes. 'Could the capable Benson not have dealt with them?'

The older woman's mouth thinned, those angry spots returning to her cheeks. 'Benson is the main cause of the problem! Indeed, personal recommendation or not, I am seriously thinking of dismissing him the moment he returns.' Her eyes now glittered with her anger. 'The servants are all in disarray without his guidance.' She had obviously forgotten her earlier reassurances to the contrary, in her agitation. 'And I am sure that there are far more guests here this evening than were actually invited.' She looked askance at the very overcrowded ballroom.

'Indeed?' Wolfingham was narrow-eyed as he also glanced at the overabundance of masked guests.

'No doubt they had heard of the entertainments here and wished to be a part of it, whether invited or not,' Clara twittered coyly.

'No doubt,' Wolfingham drawled drily. 'When Benson returns from where?' he added softly.

Clara gave an impatient shake of her head. 'He has gone to be at the bedside of his sick father. Against my instructions, I might add,' she added agitatedly. 'When he asked earlier I refused him leave to go until tomorrow, but I learnt just minutes ago that he has gone this evening anyway!'

Mariah's breath caught in her throat as she turned to give Darian a wincing glance.

Stupid!

How could they both have been so utterly, utterly stupid?

Or, perhaps more accurately, how could she and Darian have allowed themselves to become so distracted, by their ever-deepening attraction to each other, as to totally miss what had been right in front of their noses this whole time?

Of course neither Richard nor Clara Nichols had reacted as had been expected to the news that the Prince would not be attending their masked ball this evening, after all. Why should they, when neither of them was the assassin or one of the conspirators, whom Mariah and Darian had been sent here to find, in the discovered attempt to assassinate the Prince Regent.

To date, all of the known network of arrested spies, set up by André Rousseau during the year he had spent working as a tutor in England, had been employees in the households of rich or politically powerful people. Servants of one kind or another who could move about at will without attracting attention. A private secretary. A tutor. A footman.

A *butler*…

Benson!

Benson had been Rousseau's spy in the Nicholses' household.

Benson, who had only been employed in the Nicholses' household for a matter of months.

Benson, who had proved to be such 'a treasure' since coming to work in the Nicholses' household.

Benson, who *had* been the only person to leave the Nicholses' sitting room after the Prince's note had been delivered and read.

Benson, who had carried that note up the stairs to Clara Nichols's private sitting room, before no doubt proceeding to read its contents!

Benson, his suspicions perhaps aroused, who had then followed Mariah and Darian back up the stairs, before entering that passageway behind the wall in Mariah's bedchamber, for the sole purpose of listening to their conversation?

Mariah knew by Darian's slight nod of acknowledgement, and the grimness of his expression, that he had already drawn those same conclusions.

As they both must now also be aware that Benson had already departed Eton Park, before either of them had been able to make that connection.

To go where, though, and for what purpose? Did Benson intend to go to London and somehow attempt to assassinate the Prince Regent still?

'You said that Benson came to you through personal recommendation?' Wolfingham, obviously one step ahead in his thinking than Mariah, now prompted their hostess shrewdly.

'Why, yes.' Clara Nichols looked slightly surprised by his interest, before then giving an affectionate smile. 'But, of course, I could not possibly be cross with dear Wedgy. I can only assume that Benson must have fooled him as to his reliability, in the same way that he has fooled all of us.'

'"Wedgy"?' Darian had little or no patience left for the woman's prattling, especially so when she obviously had absolutely no knowledge of just how *much*, and in what way, Benson had fooled them all.

His hostess continued to smile. 'Darling Wedgy. Lord William Edgewood,' she supplied irritably as Darian continued to glower down his aristocratic nose at her. 'But I have always called him Wedgy. William and Edgewood—Wedgy, do you see?'

Darian did indeed see. He saw exactly how the slightly rotund and jolly, and apparently innocuous, Lord Edgewood, a man he now recalled was also attached to the Foreign Office and so privy to certain information—such as the Prince Regent's social engagements!—might have conspired with others in an attempt to assassinate the Prince Regent.

'We have been friends since childhood, you see,' Clara continued to confide. 'More than friends in recent years, of course,' she added coyly, obviously in reference to the debauched display of that affection they had been forced to witness the evening before. 'But I have always considered that friends make the best lovers.'

'What colour mask is Wedgewood wearing this evening?' Darian could not even pretend to listen politely to this dreadful woman another moment longer.

Clara blinked at his obvious aggression. 'He is wearing the red mask of the devil.'

How appropriate! 'And have you seen him yet this evening?'

His hostess frowned as she nodded. 'Just before this latest crisis, as it happens.'

'Where?'

Clara frowned her irritation. 'Really, Wolfingham, you are being less than polite.'

'Where did you last see him, madam?' he demanded tautly.

She blinked pale lashes. 'He was talking to one of the musicians as they prepared their instruments before they commenced playing. Why, Mariah, what on earth is wrong with Wolfingham this evening?' She looked totally bewildered as the duke turned sharply on his highly polished heels to disappear into the melee of the crowded ballroom, without so much as a word of apology or explanation.

Mariah knew exactly what was wrong with Darian, and the reason for his having left so abruptly, and her heart began to beat a wild tattoo in her chest at the realisation that Darian had every intention of confronting Lord Edgewood. 'I will explain later.' She threw the words distractedly at Clara before herself hurrying off in Darian's wake.

Very aware that the assassin's plans for this weekend had been thwarted on two levels. First, by the arrival of the Prince Regent's note of apology. And second, by Benson's hurried departure.

Whether or not Lord Edgewood knew of the disappearance of his co-conspirator, *Mariah* certainly knew that a cornered animal was more likely to come out fighting, rather than cowering in the corner. And William Edgewood, once he became aware of Benson's defection, was obviously intelligent enough to realise he no longer had anything else to lose.

A single glance at the grimness of Darian's expression, before he left to go in search of the older man, had told her that the dangerous Duke of Wolfingham fully intended to confront the older man as being the traitor he so obviously was.

As Mariah was also aware that Darian had barely survived André Rousseau's bullet just weeks ago.

* * *

'A little caution, if you please, Wolfingham!'

Darian came to an abrupt halt to turn sharply in the middle of the ballroom, having easily recognised the softly spoken warning as coming from one of his closest friends, Christian Seaton, the Duke of Sutherland. And obviously also one of those uninvited guests Clara Nichols had referred to just minutes ago!

'These masks hide a multitude of sins.' Sutherland confirmed drily, dressed similarly to Darian, in dark clothing and a black mask, his eyes glinting violet through the eye-slits. 'Your groom arrived at Winterton Manor with your note and we arrived here just in time to stop and question the Nicholses' butler as he was attempting to leave,' he supplied economically. 'Rotherham and Maystone are here somewhere, too.'

'You know of Edgewood's involvement?'

'Oh, yes. Benson squeaked like a stuck pig once he knew the game was up. No doubt hoping to shift some of the blame!' The other man gave a grim smile. 'Griff and Maystone are watching him even as we speak.'

Darian nodded abruptly. 'Do we have a plan of extraction?'

'Maystone suggests— Good heavens, what is she doing?' Sutherland growled with a sudden start of surprise.

Darian tensed, very much afraid he knew exactly which 'she' his friend was referring to. 'Where?'

'The little fool!' Sutherland had now turned fully in order to look across the heads of the other guests in the direction of the musicians. 'Can you not keep your woman under control, Darian?' he demanded disgustedly as the two of them began to push their way towards where Mariah now stood in conversation with Lord William Edgewood.

'She is not my woman—' Darian broke off with a start as he realised that, yes, that was *exactly* what Mariah now was.

His woman.

The woman he wished to protect, with his own life if necessary.

The woman he admired and respected more than any other.

The woman he now realised meant more to him than any other woman ever had. Or ever would?

And at this moment *his woman* was deliberately endangering herself by engaging in conversation with the very man they both knew to have been one of the conspirators in the intended assassination of their beloved Regent.

His mouth thinned as he prompted again, 'Do we have a plan, Christian?'

'We did, yes,' the other man confirmed just as grimly. 'That may be a little more difficult now that— Where is she going now?' Sutherland demanded incredulously, both men coming to a halt and watching helplessly as Mariah, her hand companionably in the crook of Lord Edgewood's arm, now crossed to the French doors and strolled outside on to the terrace with him.

'Damn it to hell!' Darian had never felt so helpless in his life before as he did at that moment. Or so much like putting Mariah across his knee and administering a sound thrashing, for having endangered herself so deliberately. A thrashing, because of his earlier promise to himself never to cause Mariah any physical harm, that would have to take a verbal form. A verbal tongue-lashing he fully intended to carry out the moment the two of them were alone together again.

If they were ever alone together again.

'There is such an uncomfortable crush in there already,' Mariah remarked lightly as she stepped outside into the briskness of the March evening air beside William Edgewood.

He released his arm from her hold. 'You may drop the pretence now, Countess,' he dismissed scornfully.

'Pretence?' She gazed up at him guilelessly.

Edgewood gave a scathing snort. 'I am sure that we both know, with Wolfingham so obviously your lover, that you have absolutely no real interest in stepping outside into the moonlight with an old man like me.'

In truth, Mariah had not thought any further beyond the need she felt to prevent Darian from challenging the older man, as she had known he fully intended doing when he left her side so precipitously.

Outside, and alone on the terrace with William Edgewood—who appeared to have dropped all pretence of being that amiable fool everyone believed him to be and now looked at her with shrewdly calculating eyes—she now had time and opportunity to realise her mistake.

To realise that cornered animal had now turned its rabid attentions on to her.

She faced Edgewood unflinchingly as she decided to do exactly as he had suggested and cease all pretence. 'Your cohort has already fled.'

'So Clara unwittingly informed me a few minutes ago.' He nodded tersely.

Mariah nodded briskly. 'There is no way of escaping, nowhere you might go now where you will not be caught and held for trial as a traitor and attempted assassin.'

'Would not France be the practical choice?' he derided.

Mariah gave a pained frown. 'Why? Why would you turn traitor on your own country? On your Regent?' She had once asked Martin the same question.

'You can ask me that here, in the midst of this

debauchery that has become England?' Edgewood scoffed. 'And with a Regent more licentious than the rest?'

And Martin's answer had been just the same.

'You are just as guilty of that licentiousness—'

'Necessarily so...' he nodded '...if I was to fool
others into not suspecting my real feelings on
the matter. My mother was French, you know. I
am half-French, and my loyalties lie there rather
than— Ah, Wolfingham, I wondered how long
it would take for you to follow your mistress!'
Edgewood murmured derisively as he glanced
over Mariah's shoulder. 'And I see you have
brought several of your friends with you, too!'

Mariah turned sharply to look at where Darian—and several of his friends?—had now
joined them outside on the terrace.

At least, she had fully intended to turn and
look at them.

Instead, she found herself suddenly held as
Lord Edgewood's prisoner, as he pulled her
roughly in front of him and anchored her there,
by placing an arm about her throat and pressing
a pistol painfully against her temple.

A single glance at Darian showed his eyes to be glittering intently behind his mask in the moonlight, his displeasure, at the vulnerable position in which Mariah now found herself, clear for all to see as he glared at her furiously.

She quickly moved her gaze to the three masked gentlemen standing behind him, believing she recognised one of them as being the grey-haired Aubrey Maystone, but the identity of the other two were hidden behind their masks. 'It would seem you are outnumbered, Lord Edgewood,' she remarked slightly huskily, the tightness of his arm about her throat preventing her from breathing properly.

'But I have the pistol,' he pointed out conversationally.

'We all have pistols, Edgewood,' Aubrey Maystone assured drily as those pistols now appeared in all the other gentlemen's hands.

Including Darian's, Mariah realised, wondering where on his person he could have kept it hidden until now.

Was she becoming slightly hysterical, in questioning something so trivial, when Lord Edgewood had a pistol pressed so painfully against her temple? Lord, she hoped not!

'But I also have the Countess of Carlisle,' Edgewood came back confidently. 'Eh, Wolfingham?' he added challengingly.

Darian was well aware of the fact that Edgewood now held a pistol against Mariah's temple. Could see all too clearly how the end of the barrel of that pistol was digging into her tender flesh. Hurting her.

'You are only making your situation worse, Edgewood.' Aubrey Maystone drew the other man's attention back to him.

'Could it possibly be any worse, when I am obviously already known as a conspirator and traitor against the Crown?' The other man eyed Maystone coldly.

Darian took advantage of Edgewood's distraction to inch his way slowly to the side and then forward, aided in his stealth of movement by Sutherland and Rotherham, as they both moved to flank Aubrey Maystone.

If Darian could just move a little further forward he might be able to—

'Stay exactly where you are, Wolfingham,'

Edgewood warned harshly as he now pointed the pistol in Darian's direction.

It needed only that brief moment of Edgewood's distraction from Mariah for there to be a blur of movement at Darian's side as Sutherland dived downwards towards Edgewood's legs, at the same time as Rotherham leapt forward, with the obvious intention of wrestling the raised pistol from Edgewood's hand.

Leaving Darian to stand and watch as the scene played out before him.

Mariah was deafened as Lord Edgewood's pistol suddenly went off beside her ear, quickly followed by the report of another shot being fired, before she then felt herself toppling over as Lord Edgewood's legs were knocked from beneath him, pulling her down heavily on top of him. Her last vision was of a horrified Darian before she hit her head hard on the floor of the terrace and she knew no more.

Chapter Fourteen

'I trust you know that I am still very angry with you for behaving so recklessly, madam?'

Mariah was nestled comfortably against Darian's shoulder, held securely in his arms as they travelled back to London in his ducal coach several hours later. Despite the lateness of the hour neither one of them had wished to remain at Eton Park a moment longer than they had to, once the worst of the furore had died down.

Clara Nichols had been hysterical, of course, as had many of her female guests, at learning that her friend and lover Wedgy now lay dead upon the terrace at Eton Park, a bullet through his heart.

The gentlemen present had been more prosaic regarding the situation, readily accepting Aubrey

Maystone's explanation of Lord Wedgewood having been caught in the act, by the Duke of Wolfingham, of forcing his attentions upon the Countess of Carlisle, before then being accidentally killed by his own pistol in the tussle that had followed. An act witnessed and confirmed by the Dukes of Sutherland and Rotherham.

It was far from an accurate account of the truth, of course, the fatal bullet having been fired by Aubrey Maystone himself. But none present had wished to challenge the word of men as powerful as Lord Maystone, and the Dukes of Wolfingham, Rotherham and Sutherland. And Clara Nichols had been too hysterical to question the fact that Lord Maystone, and the Dukes of Rotherham and Sutherland, had not even been invited to her masked ball.

No doubt the other woman would remember that fact once she had calmed down, but she had been far too busy enjoying being at the centre of the scandal, and the scandalous success of her masked ball, when Darian and Mariah had quietly taken their leave earlier.

The two of them had gone up the stairs to their

rooms so that Mariah might change her bloodied clothes before departing, leaving Mariah's maid and Darian's valet to pack up their things before following tomorrow.

'Mariah, you are not to fall asleep until you have listened to what I have to say!' Darian gave her shoulders a shake to prevent that from happening. 'Do you have any idea how I felt when I looked down and saw you unconscious upon the floor and covered in blood?' he demanded harshly, his impatience barely contained. 'Do you even realise that my own heart stopped beating, when I thought Maystone had missed Edgewood and had shot you instead?'

Mariah was too tired, felt too safe in Darian's arms, to care about much of anything else at the moment. 'As you see, by my presence here, he did not and I was not.'

'Mariah!'

'Darian.' She moved slightly in his arms so that she might look up at him in the lamplight, noting the dark shadows in his magnificent green eyes, the grey tinge to his tightly etched face and clenched jaw. She reached up now to gently touch that clenched jaw. 'I am safe. We are both safe.' *Darian* was safe. Which, after all, had been Mariah's only intent earlier, when she hurried across the ballroom in order to reach William Edgewood's side ahead of Darian.

Her only *interest* had been to prevent Darian from challenging the other man and perhaps being hurt or killed in the process.

Because, she had realised, she was in love with him.

She loved, and was in love with, Darian Hunter, the Duke of Wolfingham.

And strangely that realisation no longer terrified her. The emotion was no longer something for her to fear. Nor did it make her less, as she had believed loving someone would, but somehow more.

Darian now repressed a shudder. 'He might have killed you.'

She smiled. 'But he did not.'

Darian looked down at Mariah searchingly, noting the calmness of her expression and the tranquillity in those beautiful turquoise-coloured eyes.

While he was still a churning mass of emotions. Fear, for Mariah's life. Devastation, when he had believed her dead. Relief, when he had realised the blood on her gown was from Edgewood rather than her own. Elation, when she had opened her eyes minutes later and smiled at him.

Unfortunately, *all* those emotions had been followed by anger. That Mariah could have been so reckless as to have put herself in danger in the first place.

'What possessed you?' he demanded now. 'What on earth went through your mind when you deliberately placed yourself in a position of vulnerability by going outside alone on to the terrace with Edgewood?'

Her smile became rueful. 'I do not believe I was thinking much of anything at the time. It just seemed— It was the right thing for me to do, Darian.'

'It was the worst thing you could have done!' he contradicted explosively.

Her fingers rested lightly against the tautness of his cheek. 'Let us not discuss this any further just now, Darian. It is over. The Prince Regent is safe. The would-be assassins are all dead or in custody. Napoleon himself has been thwarted in his plan to devastate the alliance. It is all finally over, Darian.'

He tensed beneath those caressing fingers. '*We* are not over, Mariah!' His arms tightened about her. '*We* will never be over!'

She looked up at him quizzically. 'What do you mean?'

'Exactly as I say.' A nerve pulsed strongly in his clenched jaw. 'We have begun something this weekend, Mariah. Something good. Something wonderful. And I will not allow you to just calmly walk away from that. To walk away from *me*!'

Leaving Darian was the last thing that Mariah wanted to do. Indeed, she never wished to be apart from him ever again. Wished to spend her every waking moment with him, and her sleeping ones, too, for the rest of her life.

That was how much she had realised she loved Darian. More than life itself. More than any of the fears of love and intimacy that had plagued her for over half of her lifetime.

She looked up at him shyly beneath the sweep of her lashes. 'Did I say that I wished to walk away from you?'

'Well. No. But—' He looked nonplussed. 'It will not do, Mariah. I will not have you running all over London and putting yourself in danger as you have been doing these past few years. I will not countenance—' He broke off as she began to chuckle softly at his bluster, a dark scowl on his brow. 'I fail to see what is so funny, Mariah.'

'We are. The two of us.' She sobered as she saw that Darian was still bursting with anger. 'We are both so afraid to admit that we might care for or need anyone. In any way. Darian, I will not walk away from you once we are returned to London,' she assured him seriously. 'I will be yours for as long as you wish me to be,' she assured him huskily.

'You will?'

'I will,' she confirmed huskily. 'Of course there are still many things that need to be discussed between the two of us.' Her supposed affairs with other men being one of them. Her lack of experience in physical matters being another. 'But I am sure, once we have done so, that we will be able to come to some sort of arrangement, whereby the two of us—'

'Arrangement?' Darian repeated softly, dangerously. 'I am talking of the two of us marrying, Mariah, not forming an arrangement!'

The shock on Mariah's face at his pronouncement might have been amusing, if Darian were not so much in earnest. If he did not love this woman more than life itself. If he did not love, admire and respect Mariah more than he had realised it was possible to love, admire and respect any woman.

Except he did. Knew that he felt all of those things for Mariah. So much so that he really had thought his heart had stopped when he looked down at her earlier, covered in blood, and had thought her dead. His own life had ended, too, in those few brief moments. He had ceased to exist. Darian had ceased to live or breathe, in the belief that Mariah Beecham, Countess of Carlisle, and the woman he loved, no longer lived or breathed. All that had remained was a shell, a body, without emotions or feeling.

Until Mariah's eyes had fluttered open and she had looked up at him and smiled.

It was at that moment that Darian had decided that he was never going to let Mariah out of his sight ever again. Whatever he had to do, however long it took, he intended that Mariah would be his wife, his duchess, and at his side for the rest of their lives.

'I love you, Mariah,' he told her now, fiercely, his arms tightening about her. 'I love you and want to marry you. To spend the rest of my days and nights with you. I love you, Mariah,' he repeated determinedly. 'And however long it takes to convince you, I intend having you for my—'

'Yes.'

'—wife,' he concluded purposefully before his gaze sharpened as he realised what Mariah had said, if not why. 'Yes what?' he questioned guardedly.

'Yes, I will marry you, Darian!' She smiled up at him glowingly, tears now glistening in her eyes. 'I love you, too, my darling Darian. I love you!'

Darian continued to look down at her searchingly. Hardly daring to believe—to hope that—

'You love me? How can you possibly love me?' He frowned darkly. 'When I have been nothing but judgemental of you from the first. So disapproving. Scornful. Critical—'

'And kind, caring, protective and passionate,' Mariah spoke huskily. 'Would you prefer it if I did not love you, Darian?' she added teasingly as he still looked down at her in disbelief. 'I suppose I might try,' she continued conversationally. 'But it is so very difficult, when I believe you to be so much all of those things *I* mentioned in regard to how you are with me. I could *try* not to love you but— Darian!' She gave a strangled cry as his mouth finally claimed hers, his arms gathering her in so close against him it felt as if he was trying to make her a part of himself.

And perhaps he was, because for the next several minutes there was nothing else between them but those passionate kisses interspersed with words of love and adoration.

'I intend that we shall be married as soon as is possible,' Darian finally warned as he continued to hold Mariah tightly in his arms, as if afraid, if he let her go, she might disappear in a puff of smoke. 'I believe the least we are owed, for helping to foil this plot against the Prince Regent, is the granting of a Special Licence. Unless, of course, you would prefer to have a big grand wedding, with all of the *ton* in attendance?' he added uncertainly as the idea occurred to him that Mariah had never really had a happy wedding day. 'I suppose I might be persuaded into waiting for a few weeks longer, as long as you will allow me to spend all of my days and nights before the wedding by your side.'

'A Special Licence sounds perfect,' Mariah assured him happily. 'I have already had the big white wedding attended by the *ton*,' she dismissed huskily. 'Neither it, nor that marriage, brought me any happiness.'

'Apart from Christina.'

She gave a shake of her head. 'I have always seen Christina as somehow being apart from that marriage. As if she were only ever mine, to love and to cherish. Does that sound ridiculous, in the circumstances?'

Darian's arms tightened about her. 'Nothing you say ever sounds ridiculous to me. But I hope— I sincerely hope, would deem it an honour, if you would allow me to become another father to Christina once the two of us are married?'

Mariah's heart was already full to bursting with the love she felt for Darian, but in that moment she believed it truly overflowed with the emotion. 'I should like that very much,' she accepted emotionally. 'As, I am sure, would Christina. Martin was never a proper father to her anyway.' She frowned. 'He took as little interest in her as he did in me.'

'Carlisle was a fool.' Darian scowled. 'But his loss is my gain,' he dismissed firmly. 'I assure you that I intend telling and showing both of you, each and every day, how much you are both loved and cherished.'

'I know you will.' Mariah smiled up at him gratefully, before biting her bottom lip worriedly. 'There are still some things we need to discuss, before we make any more of these wonderful plans. Things you need to know about me—'

'No,' Darian bit out harshly.

'But—'

'I do not need to know anything more about you, Mariah, than that I love you and you love me. Nothing else matters but that,' he stated firmly.

'You have no idea how happy that makes me, Darian.' Mariah smiled tremulously. 'But these are things you really do need to know, if you are to become my husband.'

'I most assuredly am!'

'Then you *must* listen to me, Darian,' she insisted as he seemed about to deny her once again.

His jaw was tightly clenched. 'Not if you are about to tell me about the other men who have been in your life. I do not want to know, Mariah. They are unimportant, irrelevant—'

'Non-existent,' Mariah put in softly, although it inwardly thrilled her to hear Darian dismiss the existence of those lovers as being irrelevant to the two of them.

Darian's voice trailed off as he seemed to hear what she had just said, a frown between his eyes now as he looked down at her searchingly.

A searching look that Mariah returned with a steady gaze as she began to talk again. 'Seven years ago I discovered, quite by chance, that my husband was a traitor to the Crown. Let me tell all, before I lose my nerve, and then you may speak, Darian,' she pleaded as he would have interrupted once again.

'Very well.' Darian nodded slowly; in truth he was still completely stunned at Mariah's claim that she had taken no other lovers.

And so he listened. As Mariah told him of her husband's treachery to his country. Of how she had gone to London, and Aubrey Maystone, with the information. And how Aubrey Maystone had used that knowledge, and Mariah, to garner even more information from Carlisle during the last two years of that man's life. Of how she had continued her own work for the Crown for these seven years, and the sense of self and self-worth it had given her. The first she had known in her life, apart from being mother to Christina.

Darian was finally left speechless when Mariah confided in him that there had been no lovers in her life. That she had flirted, cajoled, teased information from certain gentlemen, but that she had never bedded a single one of them. That the rumour and speculation of scandal about her had grown over the years, because pride had dictated that none of those gentleman had ever wished to own to the fact that they had not been, nor ever would be, a lover to the Countess of Carlisle.

The conclusion this final revelation gave Darian was simply mind-numbing. 'Then that single, awful occasion with Carlisle, the evening Christina was conceived, was the only occasion—'

'Yes,' Mariah confirmed flatly.

'My darling!' Darian gave a pained groan. 'Then our own lovemaking—the things we did together—'

'Were utterly beautiful,' Mariah assured him firmly. 'You could not have been a more gentle, more caring, a more passionate lover, even if you had known the truth, Darian.'

Darian begged to differ. If he had known, if he had once guessed at Mariah's innocence in regard to physical love, then he would have taken things more slowly, more gently, been less physically demanding.

That Mariah had been able to respond so passionately as she had earlier today to his caresses, that she had attained her peak not once but three times, was a miracle!

Although Mariah's revelations did help to explain those puzzling moments of innocence he had sensed in her, those blushes that had seemed so out of character with the experienced siren she was reputed to be.

'I trust you are not having regrets about our lovemaking earlier today, Darian,' Mariah now teased him reprovingly. 'Because I am dearly hoping that we shall be continuing with my education, in that regard, as soon as we reach London. Christina is away until tomorrow evening,' she reminded huskily. 'And we shall have the house all to ourselves till then…'

Darian would like nothing more than to spend the night with Mariah, to make love to and with her for hours and hours without end. But he would also settle for just being in the same bed with her, of just holding her, as difficult as that might be, if she would rather wait until they were married for them to make love again.

'I would not be at all happy to wait,' Mariah answered decisively, Darian's first indication that he had spoken his reservations out loud. 'Darian, I am simply *dying* for us to make love again. I have so many years to make up for. So much I have missed. That I want to learn about and enjoy.' She curved her body seductively against his. 'You are not going to continue to deny me, are you, Darian?'

How could Darian ever deny this woman anything?

This woman whom he loved, and would always love, with every fibre of his being.

'Do you know what I thought after we had made love at Eton Park earlier today—yesterday now?' Mariah realised after a glance at the bedside clock revealed it was well after midnight, her fingers swirling in the darkness of the hair on Darian's naked chest as she leant up on her elbow beside him in the comfort of her dishevelled bed.

'Earlier today?' He arched his brows as he glanced down at their satiated and well-loved nakedness.

'Earlier today,' she insisted firmly. 'I thought, so this is what poets all write about, singers croon over and lovers will risk anything to possess. But I was wrong, Darian, because *this*, the absolute joy we have just found in each other's arms, is what poets write about, singers croon over and lovers will risk everything to possess!' Their lovemaking had been a revelation to Mariah.

She had never dreamed such pleasure existed, had never realised how wonderful it was to literally become a part of another person. To be joined to them, body, soul and heart.

To be joined to *Darian*, body, soul and heart.

'I love you, Darian,' she told him achingly, emotionally. 'I love you so very much, my darling.'

'As I love you.' His arms tightened about her once again. 'And I will love you for the rest of our lives together.'

'Promise?'

'Without a doubt. You?'

'Oh, yes!'

Mariah had absolutely no doubt it was a promise they would both cherish in their hearts and happily keep.

Epilogue

Two weeks later—Wolfingham House, London

'Was that a very despondent-looking Anthony I saw leaving just now?' Mariah prompted as she entered Darian's study.

'It was, yes.' Darian smiled as she walked across the room and straight into his welcoming arms.

She looked up at him quizzically. 'What on earth did you say to him to make him look so downhearted?'

His smile widened into a grin. 'As we had already discussed, I told him that my duchess and I had decided to give him permission to pay court to our daughter, Christina.'

After only a week of marriage, Mariah still felt a thrill in her chest at hearing herself referred to as Darian's duchess. For that was who she was now, Mariah Hunter, the Duchess of Wolfingham. How grand it sounded. And yet she knew she loved Darian so much, wanted to be with him so much, that she would have married him even if he had not been the top-lofty and wealthy Duke of Wolfingham.

Although she did not altogether trust that wicked grin upon her husband's face right now.

'If you told him that, why was Anthony looking less than happy?'

That wicked grin widened, green eyes glowing with laughter. 'Because I told him that not only does he have to win Christina's heart, but that as her stepfather, I will also expect him to prove himself as being sober and responsible, before we would agree to the match. And that even then we will not countenance there being a wedding until after Christina's eighteenth birthday.'

'What a wicked stepfather and brother you are, when you know full well that Christina has already admitted to us that she is smitten.' Mariah chuckled reprovingly.

'A little uncertainty will do my little brother

good,' Darian dismissed unrepentantly, his arms now tightening about her waist as a different sort of wickedness now gleamed in his eyes. 'Have I told you yet this morning how beautiful you look?'

'About an hour ago, I believe.' She blushed as she remembered the *way* in which he had told her.

'Have I *shown* you yet this morning how beautiful you are to me?'

'Also about an hour ago,' Mariah answered shyly.

'And would my duchess be interested in my demonstrating the depths of those feelings for her again right this minute?'

Mariah felt the thrill in her chest at just how willing she was to allow Darian to do exactly that. A thrill of excitement that now coursed hotly through the whole of her body. 'I should like to demonstrate the depth of my feelings for you first,' she suggested huskily.

Darian chuckled softly. 'Then shall we retire to the ducal bedchamber?'

The ducal bedchamber that the two of them

had shared every night before their wedding and again every night since, the two of them having decided there would be no separate bedchambers for them. Ever. That they would spend all of their nights, as well as all of their days, together.

Mariah had no idea what the future would bring. Another war to quell Napoleon was most certainly imminent. A wedding for her daughter and Anthony next year, she hoped. Perhaps a child or two of their own, for Darian and herself. A handsome boy who looked exactly like his father and a little girl, also with her father's dark hair and green eyes, so that their parents might spoil and pet them both. Mariah certainly hoped it would be so.

But she had no doubt whatsoever, that whatever the future might hold for the two of them, that they would face it together.

Always, and for ever, together…

* * * * *

Don't miss the next book in Carole Mortimer's dazzling DANGEROUS DUKES *series. Coming soon!*

23/3/2015

46 790 348 6